Elizabeth Gail

and the strange birthday party

Hilda Stahl

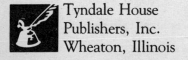

Tyndale House
Publishers, Inc.
Wheaton, Illinois

Library of Congress Catalog Card Number 79-92966
ISBN 0-8423-0724-9, paper
Copyright © 1980 by Hilda Stahl. All rights reserved.
First Printing, August 1980
Printed in the United States of America.

Dedicated with love to
Jim and Marjorie Boyer

Contents

One
Libby's
great idea

"I have it!" Elizabeth Gail Dobbs sat up in bed, her hazel eyes wide. The morning sun peeked through her bedroom window, making the pink walls brighter. "I have it!" she said louder as she flung back the pink sheet and light blanket, then leaped out of bed. Her yellow cotton nightgown touched her bony knees. Long thin arms stuck out from the sleeveless top. She smiled excitedly as she dashed down the hall. Susan would want to know. This time Susan would want to be awakened. Still, Libby hesitated at the side of Susan's bed. Maybe Susan would be angry. But Libby couldn't wait. The idea was fantastic! Before Libby completely lost her nerve she grabbed Susan's slender shoulder and shook her.

"Susan, wake up! I have it!"

Susan jerked free and covered her head with her pillow.

Libby sighed impatiently. "You will love my idea, Susan. Wake up!" Libby wanted to pull Susan out of bed or dump cold water on her. Instead Libby grabbed the pillow and jerked it away from Susan, leaving Susan's red-gold hair in tangles.

"Will you wake up, Susan? I have it!" Libby plopped on the bed beside Susan.

"Leave me alone, Libby," mumbled Susan as she tried to cover her head again.

"Susan Vera Johnson, you'll be sorry if you don't listen to me." Libby leaned close to Susan's ear. "I know how we can make money for Amy Parr."

Susan's eyes snapped open and she pushed herself up. "How? How, Libby?" Her eyes were as blue as the summer sky outside her window.

Libby hugged herself excitedly. "You and I will give birthday parties here on the farm. We can take children for wagon rides or hikes."

"And have picnics in back of the pines," chimed in Susan, her cheeks flushed with excitement. "Play games, ride horses. Oh, Libby! What a great idea!"

"I know Mom and Dad will let us have birthday parties." Libby sighed happily. "We prayed for a way to make money to help Lisa keep her baby. Now Mrs. Wilkens won't be able to make Lisa give Amy up." Libby thought of the many foster homes she'd been in during the past six years. She had not been happy or loved until the Johnson family had prayed her into their

10

home. It would be terrible if baby Amy Parr had to be placed in a foster home where she wouldn't be loved. Libby shivered. Being unloved hurt as much as the beatings she'd received from Mother.

"We'll help Lisa buy food and clothes for Amy," said Susan dreamily. "Then when Brian comes back home again he will find a happy wife and baby." Susan shook her head slowly. "I feel so sorry for Lisa. She married Brian when her parents told her not to. Now he just walked out on her. I sure hope she's right about him coming home soon. I heard Mom say that he might never come back."

Tears stung Libby's eyes and she blinked hard to keep from crying. Dad had walked out when she was three years old and she'd never seen him again. She thought of the shiny puzzle box on her desk that he'd sent her on her twelfth birthday last Valentine's Day.

Dad had been killed in a car accident, so she'd never see him again. He'd prepared the box for her before his death, and the secrets in it, along with letters from him had helped her understand him. She didn't want Amy Parr to grow up not knowing her dad.

"How will we find customers for birthday parties?" asked Susan as she squirmed around to a more comfortable position.

"We'll advertise in the newspaper like Ben does for his Christmas tree business." Libby jumped off the bed and stood with her bare feet apart, her hands clasped in front of her. "I know of someone right now who would be glad to have a party here."

Susan leaned forward eagerly. "Who?"

"Jason Thornton. He's going to be seven on Friday. Yesterday in church I heard Mrs. Thornton tell Mom that she is going crazy trying to plan a party for Jason and all his friends. We can call her and ask if we can plan the party. Mom will help us decide how much to charge." Libby could not stand still another minute. "I'm going to get dressed right now, then call Mrs. Thornton."

Susan laughed as she jumped out of bed. "Maybe you'd better wait until at least nine. She might hate getting out of bed as much as I do."

By nine o'clock Libby had finished her outdoor chores, eaten breakfast, and practiced her piano for twenty minutes. She jumped up from the piano as the grandfather clock in the hall bonged nine times. She saw Vera look up from writing a letter at her small desk. "Now can I call, Mom?"

Vera nodded with a smile. "I'm sure Barb Thornton is up by now. I'm glad you thought of having birthday parties. I know you and Susan will do a good job."

"What if she says no?" asked Libby as she picked up the telephone receiver. She looked at the note pad where she'd written the phone number when she'd first walked downstairs.

"You have to take chances when you go into

business for yourself." Vera tapped the end of the yellow ball-point pen against her hand. "Never be afraid to do something. If you never try anything, you never accomplish anything."

Libby's heart raced as she dialed the number, then waited breathlessly until Mrs. Thornton answered.

Libby licked her dry lips, then told Mrs. Thornton her plan. It was hard to breathe as she waited for the woman's answer. What if she said no? What if she laughed at the idea? Libby looked wildly around for Susan. Why hadn't Susan made the call? Mrs. Thornton would agree to Susan's plan. Maybe she wouldn't agree to any plan made by an aid kid, a kid nobody wanted. Libby took a deep breath. The Johnsons wanted her. They loved her!

"Libby," said Mrs. Thornton finally. "I think you have a wonderful idea. I'll be glad to leave it in your hands. Would twenty boys and girls be too many?"

Libby sank to the chair next to the phone. "Oh, no! Twenty would be great. We'll see you Friday at one o'clock."

"And if it rains?" Mrs. Thornton sounded as if that would be a fatal disaster.

"Then we'll have it in the basement and the kids can play games and have a cookout right in the fireplace." Libby looked quickly at Vera to see if she agreed. Vera nodded and Libby felt like laughing with delight.

Just as she replaced the receiver Libby turned

at a sound behind her. Susan stood there with her eyes round, her face pale.

"Did I hear you say twenty kids are coming?" she asked hoarsely.

"Sure."

"Twenty! And you and I are going to take care of twenty kids?" Susan pressed her hands against her cheeks. "We can't even take care of Toby and Kevin without Ben's help."

Vera laughed. "You're exaggerating, Susan. Your little brothers aren't that hard to take care of."

"We'll ask them if they want to help us," said Libby.

"I don't think they'll have time," said Vera slowly. "They're going to take care of the garden and have a vegetable stand."

Libby wanted to call Mrs. Thornton right back and tell her they'd already changed their minds, but then she remembered Amy Parr. With her pointed chin high Libby looked at Susan. "We can do it, Susan. We can have a birthday party for Jason Thornton on Friday. And it will be the best birthday party he ever had!"

Finally Susan smiled. "You're right, Libby."

Libby managed a shaky grin. She had to be right. Amy Parr needed their help.

Two
Unexpected
visitor

With a satisfied smile Libby looked down at Amy Parr, then clutched her hand to keep her from falling. Amy looked cute dressed in a little yellow shirt and a white diaper. Slowly Libby walked with Amy across the small living room floor. Amy's steps were very uncertain. She laughed and looked proudly up at Libby.

"Amy likes you, Elizabeth," said Lisa Parr, standing in the kitchen doorway.

Libby looked up with a smile. She liked to be called Elizabeth. "I think Amy's so cute. It would be fun to have a baby sister."

A strange look crossed Lisa's face and Libby wondered if Lisa was wishing that Amy were her sister instead of her baby. Libby knew Lisa was seventeen years old, but dressed as she was in blue shorts and shirt and white sandals on her feet, she looked like a little girl. Was she sorry that she'd gotten married? Did she still want to be a little girl at her mother's house?

Libby turned away and walked Amy back across the floor. Libby felt sad for Lisa. Why would Brian ever leave his wife and baby? They needed him.

"Have you signed up any more birthday parties?" asked Lisa as she sat cross-legged on the sofa.

Libby lifted Amy to her hip and walked to the sofa. "Three more people called since the ad was in Tuesday's paper." Libby turned her head to keep Amy from playing with her mouth. Amy grabbed a handful of hair and Libby had to tug it free. Finally Libby stood Amy on the floor beside the sofa. It was hard to talk with Amy in her arms.

Amy laughed and carefully walked along the sofa to play with her mother's toes.

"Oh, Amy," said Lisa, laughing as she picked up the baby and held her close. "I love you."

Libby caught her breath and looked away. Had Mother ever picked her up and laughed and told her she loved her?

"When are the parties?" asked Lisa as she handed Amy a ring of large multicolored plastic keys.

"Tomorrow we're having Jason and Saturday a boy named Gary Rousch. Monday we're having Tammy Hayes, and Tuesday a party for Megan Brovont."

"You and Susan are sure going to keep busy, aren't you?" Lisa touched Libby's arm. "I can't thank you enough for helping me. I know Brian

16

will come back soon. He has to! Then we'll pay you back every penny!"

Libby flushed. "We want to help, Lisa. And you don't have to pay us back."

"If I can help, let me know."

Libby nodded. "Megan's mother wants us to make special decorations. Maybe you can help with that."

They made plans as Amy played happily with her keys. Would Brian really come back? Libby didn't want to think about that. They had prayed that Brian would come home. God answered prayer. Libby remembered when they'd prayed for Bob DuPont to come home to Grandma Feuder so she could give him the teddy bear that she always kept on her kitchen chair. Bob had come home, then taken Grandma and Adam Feuder with him for a vacation. God answered prayer for Grandma Feuder. He would answer for Lisa Parr.

Finally Libby jumped up. "I have to go home, Lisa. I won't see you tomorrow or Saturday, but I'll see you on Sunday. If you want, Susan and I will watch Amy in the nursery at church."

"Thanks, Elizabeth, but Mrs. Taylor will be in the nursery Sunday. She doesn't like anyone in with her. Maybe another time." Lisa smiled, her blue eyes full of love. "You and Susan are wonderful to Amy and me. Thank you."

Libby ducked her head and smiled self-consciously. She mumbled good-bye again, then hurried away.

The hot sun beat down on her as she rode her bike along the road. She slowed down near the Wilkens house. Maybe Joe would be outdoors in the yard. But maybe Brenda would be. Libby made a face. She did not want to see Brenda today or hear her call her "aid kid" again. Brenda never let anyone forget that Libby was an aid kid, that she didn't really belong to the Johnsons.

No one was in the yard, so Libby peddled fast toward home. Did Joe or Brenda know that their mother was trying to have the court take baby Amy away from Lisa? What could they do if they did know? Libby frowned. Mrs. Wilkens had said that Lisa Parr couldn't support the baby, that the baby should be put in a foster home where adults who had the money and experience could take care of her. Mrs. Wilkens had to be stopped! Lisa Parr loved her baby and took good care of her. Somehow she would get enough money to take care of both of them. Libby clamped her teeth tightly. She would like to tell Mrs. Wilkens to leave Lisa alone. Mom had talked to her, but it hadn't done any good at all. Mrs. Wilkens was determined. Libby narrowed her hazel eyes and lifted her pointed chin. She was determined, too!

Libby turned into the long driveway, then stopped. She frowned. Was someone hiding behind one of the large oak trees in the front yard? Had she seen someone jump quickly out of sight? Where was Goosy Poosy? He usually honked and ran toward anyone who came in the yard. And where was Rex, the big black and tan collie?

Libby pushed down the kick stand and stood the bike to the side of the driveway. She looked toward the big white house. Had anyone looked out a window? Was she the only one who had seen someone in the yard? A shiver ran down her spine. She stood hesitantly, then walked slowly into the shade of the tall trees in the front yard. Maybe whoever hid was waiting to pounce on her and knock her out. Should she call Ben? He was stronger than she was. But if she called anyone, the person hiding would get away.

Taking a deep breath, Libby walked toward the tree where she'd seen the person. A twig snapped loudly under her foot and she jumped, staring fearfully toward the tree.

Just as she reached the tree she heard a soft sneeze. Someone was hiding on the other side of the big tree! She had not imagined it! Her heart almost leaped out of her chest. Her long legs felt too weak to hold her.

She walked around the tree and stared in surprise at a teenage girl leaning against the tree, tears running down her pale cheeks. She was dressed in blue jeans and a white tee shirt. Her long blonde hair was in wild tangles around her face and down her shoulders. Her slender hands were pressed against her mouth.

"Are you hurt?" Libby asked breathlessly. She hadn't expected anything like this.

The girl shook her head "no" while the tears continued to fall.

"Are you lost?"

Once again she shook her head.

Libby frowned. The girl looked familiar but she knew she didn't know her name or where she came from. "Can I help you?"

The girl swallowed hard. "I . . . I'm so tired and so hungry."

Libby hesitated. Should she take the girl to the house? Would Vera mind? No, she wouldn't. Vera and Chuck helped anyone who needed help. "Come with me and I'll give you some food."

The girl looked toward the house, then at Libby with a frown. "Who are you?"

Libby blinked. She should be asking the stranger who she was. Finally Libby told her her name.

"You don't live here," said the girl sharply. "The Johnsons do."

Libby flushed. "I know. But I live with them." She wanted to say she was their daughter but that wouldn't be quite true. Someday maybe they could adopt her. Someday Mother would sign the paper agreeing that she could be adopted.

The girl hesitated. "Maybe they won't want to see me. They don't know what I've done."

Nervously she pushed her tangled hair away from her face. Libby could tell by the dark shadows around the girl's eyes that she hadn't slept for a while.

"Sure, they'll want to help you," said Libby with a smile. "They're really nice."

The girl lifted her head and squared her shoulders. She stood almost a head taller than Libby. "Let's go in. I might as well let them know I'm here. I don't know what they'll say."

What was the girl talking about? Did she think that Vera would scold her for being on private property?

A horse nickered from the pen beside the barn. A rooster crowed, then the only sound was the girl's ragged breathing.

Air-conditioning was on inside the house. Libby was glad to come out of the heat and into the comfortably cool house. She opened her mouth to call Vera when Vera walked from the study, then stopped and stared at the girl beside Libby.

"Rhonda! What has happened to you?" Vera took a step toward the girl. "Why are you here?"

Libby blinked in surprise. Vera knew the girl. Suddenly Libby noticed that the girl looked like Vera. Both of them had blonde hair and blue eyes. Something about their facial expressions was the same too.

"Aunt Vera, I had to come," said Rhonda in a low voice. "I couldn't stay home another day.

I'm . . . I'm sooo miserable!" With that she flung her arms around Vera and sobbed against her neck.

Vera held the girl close, talking softly to her while Libby stared in surprise. Who was Rhonda? Where had she come from?

Three
Snowball

Libby closed and locked the gate that led to the sheep pen, then turned to Susan. "Do you suppose Rhonda was telling the truth? She acted strangely."

Susan leaned against the fence, her face sad. "She sure is upset. I couldn't believe that she'd actually run away from home. She almost fainted when Mom said she was going to call Uncle Steve and Aunt Ellen. Rhonda doesn't want them to know where she is. Oh, I wish they wouldn't get a divorce! I can understand why Rhonda couldn't decide who to live with." Susan shook her head, her red-gold pony tails bobbing. "Mom and Dad would never get a divorce! I could never decide who to live with!"

Libby shivered. That was too awful a thought! If the Johnsons ever split up she would be shoved into another foster home, and then she would never, never be loved again. She would not want to be Rhonda for anything in the world!

Susan caught Libby's arm and tugged her toward the horse barn. "We won't even think about Mom and Dad getting a divorce. They won't! Not ever! Right now let's go work with Snowball and get her used to being led. She still doesn't like to stop when you want her to."

Libby forced her mind off Rhonda's problem and thought about her white filly Snowball. How she'd grown since Libby had first seen her! It was fun to work with her and train her. Susan was very patient while she helped Libby. "Susan, I don't know if I'll ever be able to work with Snowball the way you want me to."

"You will, Libby." Susan walked beside Libby in her usual bouncy step. "Snowball has a lot of energy. You just have to let her know you're the boss. And Libby, don't ever let her nip at you the way she does."

Libby sighed. "I love her so much that I don't want to hit her."

Susan stopped and turned to Libby. "If you don't make her mind you, you'll never be able to train her right. Just remember that."

Slowly they walked to the pen. Suddenly Libby stopped. Rhonda was in the pen leading Snowball around. She was acting as if Snowball belonged to her. Libby flushed with anger. How dare Rhonda work with Snowball? Why wasn't Rhonda in the house with Vera? Maybe Rhonda thought she was here to stay! Would Vera want to keep Rhonda and get rid of Libby?

24

"Hi, girls," called Rhonda, waving happily as if she hadn't been in tears only a few hours ago. "I like Snowball. Kevin showed me around the farm and told me all the horses' names. Snowball is my favorite."

"She's mine," snapped Libby as she walked into the pen, leaving the gate for Susan to close. "I want to work with Snowball myself."

Rhonda held the halter rope out of Libby's reach. "I want to. I can do a good job. Aunt Vera won't care. She's really not yours to keep for good since you might not always live here."

The blood drained from Libby's face and her knees began to shake. It was hard to talk around the lump in her throat. "I live here. This is my home." She turned to Susan urgently. "Tell her, Susan! Tell her this is my home!"

"Don't get upset, Libby," said Susan softly. "This is your home. We're your family now. Rhonda doesn't understand." Susan turned to Rhonda. "You can work with the other horses. Let Libby work with Snowball."

Rhonda lifted her chin and looked down her nose at the girls. "I want to work with Snowball. Aunt Vera said I could do whatever I wanted. Don't be such a baby, Libby." Rhonda turned and led Snowball across the pen.

Libby clenched her fists and gritted her teeth. She wanted to dash after Rhonda and jerk the rope from her hands. Why didn't Rhonda go home where she belonged?

"Let's go to the house, Libby," said Susan as

25

she touched Libby's arm. "We'll ask Mom to talk to Rhonda about Snowball." Susan smiled. "This might help us, Libby. With the birthday parties we won't have much time to work with Snowball. Rhonda will and that'll be good for Snowball."

Libby stopped and glared at Susan. "I want Snowball to know she's mine! I don't want a strange girl teaching her! Why don't you let her work with Apache Girl? How would that make you feel?"

Susan shrugged and turned away. "You're just jealous. You don't want Snowball to like anyone but you."

Libby reached to grab Susan's hair, then stopped herself just in time. She would not be mean to Susan. She had promised the Lord that she would not be bad. Sometimes it was very hard to keep that promise. Sometimes it was impossible.

Later Libby forced herself to sound calm as she talked to Vera about Rhonda and Snowball. Vera would understand and handle the situation.

Vera dried her hands and leaned against the counter. Potatoes boiled on the stove. The good smell of meat loaf drifted from the oven. Vegetables for a tossed salad lay on the counter behind Vera. "Libby, I know how you feel. But right now Rhonda is going through a rough time. She needs something to take her mind off her problems. Can you let her work with Snowball for a while? You'll be able to when Rhonda leaves."

Libby's stomach tightened into a cold knot. How could Vera do this to her? "I don't want Rhonda to touch Snowball! She's mine!"

Vera stood straight and looked Libby right in the eyes. "Libby, this time you'll have to think of Rhonda. She needs our help and our love. I don't want you doing or saying anything that will hurt Rhonda."

For one wild minute Libby thought she would faint. How could Vera do such a thing to her? It just wasn't fair!

"How long is Rhonda staying, Mom?" asked Susan as she broke off the tip of a carrot. She crunched it loudly.

"I don't know. I tried to call Steve, but there was no answer." Vera shook her head. "That brother of mine needs someone to have a very serious talk with him. I'm shocked that he's thinking of divorce."

"I hope Rhonda leaves tomorrow," said Libby sourly. "I don't want her here."

Vera slipped her arms around Libby. "You know how it feels to think no one cares for you. That's the way Rhonda is feeling now. Please, be patient with her."

Libby looked at Vera, then quickly down. "I'll try." Oh, but it would be hard! "Can't you tell her to stay away from Snowball?"

Vera sighed. "I could, Libby, but I won't. She

found something to do to keep herself occupied, something that she enjoys doing. Let her work with Snowball. She's good at training horses. Be thankful for her help."

Libby wanted to scream. Slowly she turned and walked out of the kitchen. She would have to obey Vera, but she would not like it. And she would not like Rhonda or be nice to her.

Susan grabbed Libby's arm just as she started up the wide stairs. "Don't be mad, Libby. We've got a lot of work to do and it'll be nice to have Rhonda take care of Snowball."

Libby jerked free and glared at Susan. "Leave me alone! Go talk to your cousin!"

Susan stamped her foot. "You're acting like a big baby! Go away and pout if you want, Libby, but I'm going to get those prizes wrapped for Jason's party tomorrow. Here it was your idea and you don't even want to help!" Tossing her head, Susan turned and walked into the family room to the table where they'd laid out wrapping paper and gifts.

The steady rhythm of the grandfather clock's tock-tock sounded loud in Libby's ears. She clutched the shiny banister. She wanted to run to her room and cry against Pinky, her pink fuzzy dog that sat on her bed. But she couldn't leave all the work for Susan to do.

Slowly Libby walked into the family room and sat across the table from Susan.

"I'm glad you're not mad anymore," said Susan with a grin.

Libby took a deep breath. "I'm sorry for talking mean to you, Susan. We'll work together so we can be ready for Jason's birthday party."

Quietly they wrapped gifts. Just as Libby sat the last one in the big box on the floor at her feet, Kevin burst into the room. His eyes looked wide and scared behind his glasses. His chest heaved up and down under his tee shirt.

"Rhonda's beating Snowball!" he cried. "I told her to stop but she wouldn't!"

Libby leaped to her feet and raced from the room. She heard Susan and Kevin right behind her. How dare Rhonda beat Snowball!

The hot sun almost blinded Libby as she ran to the pen. Would Snowball be dead? Libby stopped at the gate. Rhonda was leading Snowball around and around. Snowball was not hurt. She acted as if she was having fun! Libby frowned at Kevin.

"She was beating her!" cried Kevin as he climbed on the bottom board of the white fence.

Rhonda led Snowball to stand in front of Libby. "I didn't beat Snowball. I had to hit her because she was nipping me."

Just then Snowball reached out and nipped Libby on the arm. Libby jumped back and Rhonda slapped Snowball and firmly told her to stop nipping. Libby wanted to slap Rhonda.

"You'll ruin Snowball if you allow her to have her way," said Rhonda as she stroked the filly's white face.

"Don't hit her again!" Libby reached for the

lead rope but Rhonda held it out of reach.

"You're not firm enough with her," said Rhonda. "I'm going to ask Uncle Chuck if I can be in complete charge of her while I'm here this summer."

Libby started over the fence after Rhonda but Susan grabbed her and held her back.

"We'll talk to Dad as soon as he gets home, Libby."

Libby leaned weakly against the fence. Chuck wouldn't let Rhonda train Snowball, would he? And did Rhonda mean to stay the entire summer?

Four
The first party

Libby sank down on the red hassock in her bedroom and covered her face with trembling hands. Chuck had said that Rhonda could train Snowball! He had said Rhonda would do a better job!

"You have a very soft heart for animals, Elizabeth," Chuck had said last night in his study when Libby had gone to talk with him. "But right now Snowball needs a firm hand, not a soft heart. Rhonda has trained many, many horses. She knows what she's doing. I know it'll be hard on you since Snowball is yours. But, Elizabeth, this is for the best."

Libby had tried talking to Chuck again before he went to work at his store in town, but he'd been firm. How could she face the new day?

With a moan Libby lifted her face and shook her head. Chuck had never hurt her before. Had he stopped loving her? Didn't he want her anymore? Rhonda was *real* family! She had stepped in. Now Chuck thought only about her. Libby clasped her hands together. It was going to be very hard to have the birthday party for Jason and pretend that she was happy and cheerful. Libby rubbed her hands down her jeans. Chuck had often told her to give her problems to Jesus and let him take care of them. She could not stand the hurt she felt. She could not work with the kids at the birthday party unless she felt better.

Libby closed her eyes and quietly talked to Jesus. Tears slipped down her cheeks. As she prayed she felt the hurt leave. She could almost smile. Jesus would help her all day long. He loved her! He was with her every minute.

With a big sigh Libby walked to the mirror to brush her hair. She must hurry because she and Susan had several things to do before Jason and his friends came. Libby's heart suddenly leaped with excitement. Today was the first day of the birthday parties! Today they would have money to give Lisa for Amy.

Ben had agreed to help them for a while. He'd said that he and Kevin and Toby had used the Rototiller in the garden and they were caught up with their work. Kevin and Toby would help with the pony rides.

Just then Susan rushed into Libby's bedroom. "I'm so nervous, Libby! I don't know if I can work with you today!" Susan grabbed Libby's arm. "I don't know what's wrong with me."

Libby laughed. "Susan, you've helped with parties that Mom had for Sunday school classes and school classes. You're just worried because we've planned this. You'll see, Susan, it will be great! And think of the money we can give to Lisa. She'll be able to buy some things for Amy."

Susan gulped hard, then took a deep breath. She tucked her pale green shirt into her dark green jeans. "You're right, Libby. I'm fine now."

"Let's go see if Ben has Jack and Dan hitched to the wagon." Libby hurried downstairs with Susan beside her. "The kids will love the wagon ride. Some of them have never ridden in a wagon pulled by big draft horses before." Libby remembered her first look at the matched gray team. She had never seen such big horses. For a while she'd been a little afraid of them but they were very gentle and instantly obeyed every command, so she'd lost all her fear.

"The cake is beautiful, girls," said Vera with a wide smile as the girls stopped in the kitchen. "I think Jason will be pleased."

Libby gasped in delight as she looked at the big cake. The blue and white frosting was decorated with circus animals on toothpicks. Seven candles stood on the cake. Besides the large cake Vera had baked twenty cupcakes and decorated them.

"I put a candle on each cupcake so that each child will be able to blow one out," said Vera as she studied her work. "And if they don't eat the cupcakes here, they can take them home."

"Thanks, Mom," said Susan, hugging Vera tightly.

"Thank you very much," said Libby, hugging Vera after Susan. Vera smelled like vanilla. Her blonde hair tickled Libby's face. Libby couldn't picture Mother baking birthday cakes or being nice or smelling like vanilla.

Several minutes later Libby and Susan went over beside the big wagon. Jack and Dan stood patiently in the harness, waiting to give rides.

Libby smiled at Ben. She thought he looked wonderful dressed in a blue short-sleeved pullover shirt and blue jeans. His red hair had been cut the day before and was in nice order. His hazel eyes sparkled with excitement.

"Your idea for birthday parties is a good one, Elizabeth," said Ben. "We could have birthday parties all year long if we wanted. As soon as the garden produce is sold, I could help you a lot."

"Thanks, Ben." Libby puffed up with pride. She was glad Ben liked her idea and that he was willing to help later.

Just then Kevin called to her from the pen where they were going to give rides on Sleepy and Dusty. Libby ran to the pen and watched as Toby rode Dusty across the pen. He could ride well already. His red hair flopped up and down. The freckles on his face seemed to stand out more in the bright sunlight.

"When will they get here?" asked Kevin as he pushed his glasses against his nose. His blond hair was damp with perspiration.

"Soon, I think," said Libby. She leaned against the fence and reached through to pet Sleepy. He looked too sleepy to take kids for rides today. "I'm glad you and Toby are helping us."

Kevin leaned close to whisper to Libby. "Rhonda hit Snowball again! I saw her and I told her to stop. She said for me to mind my own business. I wish she would've stayed home where she belongs. I sure wouldn't let her hit Sleepy."

A cold knot settled in Libby's stomach. She didn't want Rhonda hitting Snowball, but Chuck had said that Snowball was headstrong and needed a firm hand. He said that when he'd trained Tessy, Snowball's mother, he'd had to use a very firm hand and hit her often. He had told Libby to let Rhonda have her way with Snowball without interfering. Oh, but it was hard! "I can't help what your cousin does, Kevin," said Libby sharper than she'd meant to. She saw the hurt look on his face but she felt too bad to apologize just then.

A blue and white van drove into the long driveway. Goosy Poosy honked loudly from the chicken pen where Kevin had put him during the time the party would be going on. Goosy Poosy was too big to be allowed to push against such little children. He could easily knock them down and frighten them. Libby remembered the time when she'd first come to live at the Johnson farm. The big white goose had scared her badly, even knocked her down. She didn't want any visitor frightened away because of the goose.

Susan called to Libby and they walked to meet Mrs. Thornton as she opened the doors. Boys and girls piled out. Suddenly twenty children looked more like one hundred and twenty to Libby. How noisy they were!

Libby caught Jason's hand. "Happy birthday, Jason." All the children stopped shouting and listened and watched. "This is your day, Jason. We have some wonderful surprises for you." Libby pointed to Jack and Dan, hitched to the big farm wagon. Chuck had placed bales of hay in the wagon so that all the children could ride at once.

As Libby explained what they would do first, Susan lined up the children. And when Libby nodded, Susan led them in a follow-the-leader game that got out all the energy that they'd stored up in the car ride from town. Finally she led them to the big wagon and stood back with Libby as twenty children scrambled into the wagon. Mrs. Thornton sat toward the back with Jason beside her. Susan sat with Ben and Libby climbed in between two small girls who looked frightened. She talked quietly to them until they relaxed, then actually smiled. Libby liked the gentle sway of the wagon. She was glad Ben could handle Jack and Dan so well. It would be terrible if they ran away. Chuck had trained the matched grays himself. They were very well-mannered. Chuck wouldn't allow a mean-tempered horse on the farm.

As they rode past the cattle pasture, Libby spotted three people walking into a grove of trees. She frowned. Who would trespass on the Johnson's farm? As she watched them the shortest one of the group turned and looked right at Libby. He was a brown-haired boy about her age, maybe a little older. He frowned, then ducked his head as he turned and disappeared into the trees. The two other people didn't turn or make themselves known as Ben drove past them. Chuck would want to know about them.

Soon Libby forgot about the trespassers when Ben pulled to a stop and the children scrambled out to find their hidden treasures. Libby had explained to them where to look.

"Come back to the wagon when you find the treasure with your name printed on it." Libby wondered if they heard her, then shrugged. They were so excited about being in the country and hunting a treasure that they wouldn't hear anything.

Mrs. Thornton joined Libby beside the wagon. "Libby, I know that Jason will always remember this birthday party. Thank you. I could not have done it myself. You saved me hours of work." She turned to Susan. "You girls will have more customers than you'll know what to do with."

"We hope so," said Susan. She swatted a fly away from her ear.

Just then Jason called to his mother and she

hurried to his side. Libby turned to Susan.

"Did you see those people walking in the pasture?" she asked urgently.

Susan nodded with a frown. "Dad won't like that a bit. I wonder what they were doing."

Ben spoke from beside the horses. "They looked suspicious to me. And even when I slowed down and gave them a chance to come talk to us, they stayed out of sight in the trees. I wonder what they were up to."

Libby didn't have time to think about it. The children rushed back, excitedly waving their treasures and shouting noisily. They climbed back in the wagon and the ride continued.

By the end of the party Libby didn't know who was more tired, herself and Susan or the children. The cake had been enjoyed by everyone. Ice cream had disappeared quickly. Having the children march to the garbage can with their paper plates and cups had worked perfectly.

"Happy birthday, Jason," said Libby with a smile as he wearily followed the other children into the van. "Come again next year."

"I will! Thanks, Libby. Thanks, Susan."

Several of the children shouted out the windows, saying that they would come for their birthdays.

It seemed very quiet as Libby watched the van back out of the driveway and turn toward town. Goosy Poosy honked, then was quiet. Maybe he was glad for the silence.

38

Susan hugged Libby, then stood back with a wide smile. "We're really in business, Libby."

"Our first birthday party was a big success," said Libby proudly. "We have money for Amy Parr. I can't wait to see Lisa and give it to her."

"Maybe Brian will be home today," said Susan as she picked up a napkin that the wind had blown off the table.

"Maybe," said Libby, then stopped herself. "We asked the Lord to send him home. Brian *will* come home." Libby locked her fingers together tightly. For Lisa and for baby Amy, he just had to come home!

Five
A strange party

Libby hurried outdoors. It was time for Gary Rousch and his parents to come for Gary's birthday. His mother had said he was turning thirteen and that eight people were coming. Libby sighed in relief. Eight would be much easier to handle than twenty!

Ben ran up to her, puffing hard. "I'm sorry, Elizabeth. I forgot the time. Joe and I were watching the races at his house and I forgot about hitching up Jack and Dan."

For one wild minute Libby thought she was going to hit Ben, then she took a deep breath and closed her eyes tightly. It wouldn't take that long, and if the Rousch party came before Ben was done she and Susan could show them around. They had said they were very interested in the farm.

"Are you all right, Elizabeth?" asked Ben in concern. Nervously he pushed his red hair off his wide forehead.

Libby managed a smile. "I'm fine, Ben. I'll help you harness the horses and Susan can watch out for the Rousch party." Libby looked around for Susan. Where was she? Had she forgotten, too? Libby shivered even though the sun was very hot. Goosy Poosy honked and ran toward Libby, his long white neck out and his wings flapping. Libby jumped behind Ben and the goose rubbed his neck against Ben.

"Why didn't Kevin lock Goosy Poosy in the chicken pen?" asked Libby sharply. She looked around for Kevin. He wasn't in the horse pen and neither was Toby. Where was everyone?

"Kevin!" shouted Libby with her hands cupped around her mouth. Her short brown hair felt hot and damp. "Kevin! Toby! Where are you?"

She waited. There was no answer. She watched Ben run to the horse barn for Jack and Dan. She shouted again. Finally she rushed into the house. She found the boys and Susan in the family room watching cartoons on TV. Libby wanted to stamp her foot in rage. Didn't they know it was time for the birthday party?

Susan glanced up, then leaped guiltily to her feet. "I just wanted to see the end of the program," she said with a sheepish grin. "Is it time?"

"Yes," snapped Libby. "Kevin, lock up Goosy Poosy."

Kevin looked around with a frown. "You do it, Libby. I can't miss the end."

Libby doubled her fists at her sides. "Kevin, you do it! I'll tell Mom if you don't."

"Be quiet," said Toby, scowling. "I can't hear the TV."

Libby rushed over and clicked off the TV. She stood right in front of it. "It's time for the party and we are not ready."

"Turn it on!" cried Toby and Kevin together. "It's not over yet."

Susan touched Libby's arm. "Calm down, Libby. We'll get everything ready on time. I'm sorry for not helping like I should have."

Libby let out her breath in a rush. "I guess I'm nervous. I want it to turn out just right. It's different planning a party for a thirteen-year-old than it is for a seven-year-old."

Kevin started for the door. "I'll lock up Goosy Poosy. Toby, you saddle Sleepy and Dusty."

Toby made a face, then finally agreed. He tugged his tee shirt over his blue shorts as he followed Kevin out.

The grandfather clock bonged one o'clock. Libby jumped, her hand at her mouth, her eyes large. It was time and she wasn't outdoors to meet the party. She rushed out the front door with Susan close behind. A small dark blue car pulled in the driveway and around back. Libby dashed around after it. She had seen only three people in the car. Maybe they weren't the people she was expecting. Or maybe someone else would drive the others.

A man of medium height walked around the

42

car to meet Libby. The wind ruffled his brown hair. His pants and shirt looked too big for him, giving him an unkempt appearance. His voice as he greeted Libby grated against her ears. He introduced himself as Pete Rousch, his wife as Lorraine, and his son as Gary. Libby greeted them, then stared in surprise at the boy. He was the same boy who had been trespassing yesterday when they'd taken Jason and his friends on the wagon ride. For a minute she was speechless, then she asked Mr. Rousch about the other guests.

"We're the only ones who could come," he answered gruffly. "That won't matter to you none. We're still paying what you asked." He pulled out his wallet and shoved the bills into her hands. "Let's get on with it."

Libby stared at Susan. Three people instead of eight! Libby licked her lips nervously. They wouldn't want to go for a wagon ride or follow a map through the pines and Christmas trees. "Do you ride, Mr. Rousch? We could trail ride if you want."

Just then Ben walked into sight leading Jack and Dan hitched to the big farm wagon.

"We'll go in that," said Mr. Rousch, pointing to the wagon. "Any objections?" He almost glared at Libby and she wanted to call the whole thing off and give back his money.

"We can take a wagon ride." Libby walked slowly toward the wagon. Did Ben recognize these people as the trespassers from yesterday?

How could she find out? Libby looked questioningly at Ben. She could see by his expression that he did recognize them. He opened his mouth to say something, then closed it.

Mrs. Rousch touched Libby's arm. She was just a little taller than Libby and was dressed in cotton pants and a sleeveless blouse. Her black hair was held back by a yellow band the color of her blouse. "We don't mind going for a ride on our own. Since the other kids didn't show up we won't trouble you none. Just stay home and let us take your horses for a nice ride around your farm."

"We like going," said Ben before Libby could speak. "We'll go with you and make it seem more like a real party."

"What do you mean 'real' party?" asked Mr. Rousch sharply, his brows almost meeting over his large nose.

Libby stepped closer to Ben. Were these people trouble for them? "He just meant the more the merrier," said Libby as she forced a smile. She saw the man relax. Libby looked quickly toward the house. Should she run to tell Vera about these people? Maybe Gary Rousch had been with two others yesterday. She looked at him, then quickly away. He had been studying her. Did he know that she'd seen him enough yesterday to recognize him? Why had he been trespassing?

As they climbed in the wagon Libby heard

44

Mrs. Rousch whisper something to her husband. He looked quickly at Libby, then frowned at his wife and motioned for her to be quiet.

The wagon swayed along just as it had yesterday but there was no laughter and no shouts. Libby moved closer to Ben. She couldn't say anything to him for fear of the others hearing. Susan sat just in back of Libby. Mr. and Mrs. Rousch sat with Gary at the back of the wagon. Gary did not smile. He didn't act like the birthday boy should act on a special birthday party.

"Stop here," commanded Mr. Rousch as Ben drove through the cattle pasture.

Libby's heart raced. This was here they'd seen them yesterday. She shivered as Ben pulled to a stop.

"We want to look at the wild flowers growing in those trees," said Mrs. Rousch as she stood up. "Our hobby is studying wild flowers. You children can wait right here in the wagon. We'll be back shortly." She jumped down with her husband and son beside her.

Libby stared at Ben and Susan. What a strange birthday party! Why would Mr. Rousch pay her to have a party for Gary if he didn't want to do the planned activities. Were they really interested in wild flowers?

"They are weird," whispered Susan as she huddled close to Libby and Ben.

"I think they're looking for something," whispered Ben thoughtfully. "See the way they're walking and looking down. Wild flowers aren't that hard to spot."

Birds flew from the trees. A cow mooed. Libby climbed from the wagon, her hazel eyes wide. "I think we should join them. Dad wouldn't want them walking by themselves."

Susan jumped down beside Libby. "I don't think they want us with them. They might get mad and yell at us or worse." She shivered and pressed her arms across her chest.

Ben shoved his hands into his pockets and hunched his thin shoulders. He and Libby were about the same height. Susan stood almost a head shorter. "Susan, you stay with the wagon. Elizabeth and I will follow the Rousches."

"I don't want to stay here by myself," cried Susan urgently.

"Why?" asked Ben with a frown. "You aren't scared, are you?"

She shrugged and grinned sheepishly. "Just a little."

"We'll be right over there," said Libby, pointing. She could understand how Susan felt. She was just a little scared too.

Slowly Libby and Ben walked across the pasture to the trees. Gary was walking behind his parents. His shoulders drooped as he walked as if he were carrying something heavy. Libby could tell he was very unhappy. She knew a lot about unhappiness.

The Rousches disappeared in the trees and Libby quickened her steps. Why did she feel this urgent need to hurry and catch up with them? Maybe they were dangerous. Or maybe they really were hunting wild flowers.

Ben touched her arm and stopped her. "Elizabeth," he whispered as he looked quickly toward the trees. "Let's just walk quietly without letting them know we're coming. Maybe we'll learn something."

Ben suspected something too! Libby wanted to grab his hand and hang on tightly. She looked back at the wagon where Susan stood, waiting safely near Jack and Dan. Why hadn't Susan walked with Ben? Libby took a deep, shaky breath. Desperately she wanted to be standing at the wagon waiting instead of following strangers into the woods. Why had she thought of having birthday parties? What a dumb idea!

Ben nudged her and motioned for her to walk with him. Her legs felt like rubber as she walked into the trees. She jumped as a small animal scurried in the underbrush. She stopped when Ben did and listened. For a minute the movements of animals were the only sound, then Libby heard voices. The Rousches were arguing. Libby couldn't make out what they were saying. Maybe she and Ben should go back to the wagon. Maybe the Rouches were having a family fight.

Slowly, reluctantly Libby walked ahead with Ben. Were they walking into danger? Chills ran up and down her spine. There was no danger! Why was she letting her imagination run wild?

Six
Gary Rousch

Libby pressed tightly against a large oak, her hazel eyes wide, her heart racing frantically. Ben stood just to her left behind another tree. Was he frightened too?

Pete Rousch's sharp voice nearby made Libby want to run back to the wagon with Susan. Libby held her breath and forced herself to listen.

"Act your age, Gary," snapped Pete Rousch. "Help us look before those smarty kids run over here to walk with us."

Libby blinked and swallowed hard. She looked at Ben. He looked very pale. Maybe it was just because they were in the shadows of all the trees. A mosquito buzzed around her head and she didn't dare swat at it. What were the Rousches looking for?

"I wanna go home," whined Gary. "It's hot and I'm thirsty."

Libby thought about the big jug of fruit punch

she'd made for the party. It would take a while to drink it all.

"I found something!" cried Lorraine Rousch. Libby wanted desperately to peek around to see what Lorraine Rousch had found.

"It's nothing," snapped Pete impatiently. "Look. It has faded writing on it. It's only an old math paper."

Libby's heart leaped. They were looking for a paper of some kind. But why? And what would be that important on a paper that they'd have to look for it?

"I'm not gonna look anymore," said Gary. "I'm going back to the wagon. I'm getting all bit up by mosquitoes."

Libby looked wildly at Ben. For once he looked startled.

"You're not going anywhere until I say you are," snapped Pete. "Help me look over there. I saw him hide something in this area. We got to find it. You know what it would mean if someone else found it."

Libby moistened her lips with the tip of her tongue. Who had hidden what? She looked at Ben and he jerked his head to tell her they should get out of there.

She backed slowly away from the tree. Suddenly her heel caught on something and she started to fall. She bit her tongue and almost cried out with pain. Her arms flailed wildly and she would have fallen but Ben grabbed her. Oh, what a lot of noise they'd made!

"Mr. Rousch," called Ben. "Where are you?" Then whispered to Libby, "They heard us."

Libby's body was wet with perspiration. With Ben calling out like that they would think she and Ben had just walked up. Maybe! But what if they suspected that they'd listened?

Libby rubbed the back of her leg where she'd been poked with the stick she'd tripped on. She looked down, then stared in surprise. A stick poked out of the ground. At the base, lying on the ground, was a large ring with a round red stone in it. It looked like Chuck's class ring from high school. Quickly Libby slipped it off the stick and dropped it in her pocket just as the Rousches walked around the trees. She saw the anger on the man's face. The woman looked tired and hot and the boy relieved.

"We wanted some time to ourselves on our boy's birthday," snapped Pete Rousch, scowling at Ben. "You two go back to the wagon and wait for us."

"But we have lots of things planned," said Libby, surprised that her voice could sound so normal. "And back at the house we have cake and ice cream and punch." She saw the look on Gary's face and knew he wanted to eat.

"I paid for this party and I'll have the say about it," said Pete impatiently. "If I say we want a family time together, then we get it. You two go back to your wagon."

"I'm hot," whined Gary. He pushed his hair back from his face. "I want to go." A triumphant

50

look crossed his face. "It's my birthday. I should get to do what I want. And right now I want a drink of iced cold punch."

Libby thought Pete's blood vessels would rupture. Cords stood out on his neck. His face turned a dark red. He doubled his fists until the veins popped out in his hands. Did Gary know his father was very, very angry? Gary didn't seem to care.

"What plans did you have?" asked Gary, looking at Libby. "I want to hear them so I can decide if I want to do them."

Pete grabbed Gary's arm and gripped it tightly. Gary's face turned gray and he tried to get away.

"I'm the boss. Remember that!" Pete pushed his face down close to Gary's. "Don't get smart with me, kid. You'd be very sorry. We'll do what I say we'll do."

Lorraine Rousch looked quickly at Libby and Ben, then touched Pete's arm. "Don't hurt the boy, Pete. He wants his birthday party to be fun."

Libby heard the way she stressed "birthday party." To Libby's surprise, Pete released Gary and apologized to him in a very nice manner.

Lorraine laid a soft hand on Gary's arm. She smiled down at him. "Are you sure you wouldn't want to look around these woods for more flowers? We could hike around just a little longer, then go back and have cake and ice cream."

Libby knew Gary would refuse, then she saw

fear on his face and was very surprised to hear him agree with Lorraine.

Lorraine smiled sweetly at Libby and Ben. "Why don't you join us? We are looking for tiny wild flowers. I found the red ones that grow on moss. Would you like to help us look?"

Libby glanced at Ben. The woman sounded so sincere, so truthful.

"We'll help you," said Ben, nodding his red head.

A shiver ran down Libby's spine as she nodded yes. She wanted to walk over to Gary and tell him she'd help him. She recognized Gary's fear because of Mother. Mother had always caused Libby to fear. Did Lorraine Rousch beat Gary? Did she lock him in a dark closet without food or water for a day at a time? Had she ever told him she'd be right back, then left him for days and days?

Suddenly the fear engulfed Libby and she wanted to turn and run and run. For one wild minute Lorraine looked just like Marie Dobbs, Libby's mother.

"What's wrong, Elizabeth?" asked Ben anxiously.

Libby stared at him, then grabbed his hand and clung to it with all her strength. Lorraine was not Mother! Libby tried to say something to Ben but the words would not come. She had nothing to fear! Mother was in Australia. Mother could not hurt her!

"I think we should go home," said Ben

anxiously. He turned to the others. "Elizabeth isn't feeling well. We have to go home right now."

Libby shivered. Chuck had said that fear was not from God. Chuck had said that Satan likes to put fear on Christians to keep them in bondage. Libby had to find Chuck to pray with her to get rid of her fear! As they walked back to the wagon Libby half heard the grumbling and complaining from Pete Rousch. She knew Gary was relieved. But would her actions get Gary into trouble later?

"I was getting worried about you," said Susan, her face white, her blue eyes wide.

"We're going back to the house now," said Ben as he climbed in the wagon. Jack and Dan shook their harness and nickered. They were ready to go home, too.

Libby sat beside Ben with her hands gripped tightly in her lap. How could she help Gary Rousch?

Ben called for the horses to get up. The wagon jerked, then swayed gently as Jack and Dan turned and headed for home. Ben laid his hand on Libby's clenched hands. "Don't be afraid," he whispered.

She jumped, then stared at him. "I can't help it," she whispered painfully.

"Dad says we don't have to accept fear," whispered Ben close to Libby's ear. "You have to speak to fear in Jesus' name and command it to leave you."

53

Libby pressed close to Ben. Dare she do what he said?

"What're you kids whispering about?" growled Pete Rousch from the back of the wagon where he was sitting with Lorraine and Gary.

Ben turned his head. "Sit back and enjoy the ride. We'll be home in a little while." He turned back to Libby. "Don't be afraid of them."

"What's wrong?" whispered Susan from behind Libby.

"We'll talk later," whispered Ben.

Libby stared at the horses' ears as she thought about what Ben had said about fear. She would do it! She could not allow fear to possess her this way. She belonged to Jesus. He didn't want her to be afraid. "Fear," whispered Libby, "you have to leave in Jesus' name. I will not fear! I will trust Jesus." Suddenly the fear was gone.

Libby turned to Ben with a wide, relieved smile. "I'm all right now, Ben. Jesus took away my fear." She wanted to say a lot more but she knew the Rousches were already impatient and angry. She looked back at them, caught Gary's eye, and smiled at him. Could she tell him that Jesus loved him and wanted to take away his fear?

Gary jerked his head around and pretended to be interested in the barn as they drove into the farm yard. Libby wondered what he was thinking.

A few minutes later Ben led Jack and Dan toward the barn and Libby with Susan beside her

54

asked the Rousches to have a seat at the picnic table in back of the house.

"We'll serve the birthday cake and ice cream out here." Libby smiled.

"We don't have time," snapped Pete Rousch as he grabbed Gary's arm. "We are going home right now."

"But what about the birthday cake?" asked Susan in a puzzled voice.

"We don't want it," snapped Pete, frowning. "Eat it yourselves."

"I want to stay," said Gary as he pulled back from Pete.

"We will go now!" Lorraine narrowed her blue eyes and stood with her hands on her hips. "Get in the car, Gary."

Libby shivered as Gary ran to the car, his face gray.

Susan stood quietly beside Libby until they drove away. "They sure paid a lot of money for nothing."

Libby reached in her pocket for the bills Pete had stuffed in her hand. She touched something hard, then pulled out the ring she'd found.

"Where'd you get Dad's class ring?" asked Susan sharply as she looked at the ring on Libby's palm.

Libby picked it up and studied it closely. "It's not Dad's ring, Susan. Look at the date on it. This belongs to someone who graduated two years ago. How did it get on our property?"

"Where did you find it?" Susan reached for the

ring and studied it carefully. She looked inside, then gasped. "Libby! Libby, look at the name inside."

Libby looked, her heart thudding. "Brian Parr. The ring belongs to Brian Parr!"

Seven
A letter
from Mark

"What did you say about Brian Parr?"

Libby looked up with a gasp. Brenda Wilkens stood just a foot away from Libby and Susan. Brenda was dressed in yellow shorts and tank top with white sandals on her feet. Her long black hair was in two braids that hung over her slender shoulders. Libby wanted to walk into the house, away from Brenda.

"Don't just stand and stare at me, aid kid," snapped Brenda, standing with her hands on her hips, her dark eyes boring into Libby's. "I want to know what you said about Brian Parr."

"So you can tell your mother?" Libby slipped the ring into her pocket before Brenda could see it.

"Your mother should mind her own business," said Susan sharply. "She shouldn't try to take Amy away from Lisa."

Brenda shrugged. "What my mother does is no business of yours." Brenda held up an envelope. "The mailman put this in our box by accident. It's for you, Susan." Brenda grinned and lifted her dark eyebrows. "It's from Mark McCall in Nebraska."

Libby's heart leaped. Mark McCall had promised to write to her when they'd left Nebraska in June. But Brenda had said the letter was addressed to Susan. Why hadn't Mark written to her? Libby wanted to grab the envelope out of Susan's hand and rip it open. How were Mark and his family? How was Old Zeb? "Read your letter, Susan," snapped Libby, pushing her hands deep into her jeans pockets so Susan wouldn't see how they trembled.

"Where is *your* letter from Nebraska, aid kid?" asked Brenda with a sneer. "Ben told Joe and me all about your visit and about Mark McCall."

Susan pressed the letter to her heart and sighed happily. "I'm going to my room. I'll be back after I read my letter."

Libby watched jealously as Susan ran into the house with her letter. Why hadn't Mark written to her? Was it because she was ugly? Susan was short and slender and very pretty. Mark probably liked short, pretty girls, not tall, thin, ugly girls.

"What a cry baby you are, aid kid," said Brenda, flipping her braid over her shoulder.

Libby blinked hard. She would not cry! Especially not in front of Brenda Wilkens!

"I thought you had a birthday party planned

for today." Brenda looked around with a frown. "I sure don't see any kids."

"They already left." Libby took a deep breath. She would try her best not to be rude to Brenda.

Libby almost laughed aloud with relief when Ben walked out of the barn. With Ben around, Brenda would ignore her.

"Hi, Ben," said Brenda with a warm smile. "Want to go bike riding with me? I know the party is over and you don't have to do chores for a while. It's a nice day for bike riding."

Ben looked quickly at Libby, then at Brenda. "I guess I can go."

Libby wanted to scream at Ben. Why was he always so nice to Brenda? No matter how mean she got, he still liked her. Did he like her because she liked him so much?

"Elizabeth, tell Mom I'll be back in a little while."

Brenda looked triumphantly at Libby, then walked away with Ben beside her to her bike near the driveway. Libby watched Ben climb on his bike and ride with Brenda down the driveway, then onto the road toward the big white house.

Goosy Poosy honked from the chicken pen. Slowly Libby walked to the pen and opened the gate. Goosy Poosy honked loudly, then half ran, half flew out of the pen into the yard. Libby giggled. Goosy Poosy was glad to be free again. He thought he was too good to be locked up with the chickens.

Rex barked and pulled against his chain. Libby walked across the yard to his dog house and knelt down beside him, burying her face in his long black and tan fur.

"My day is ruined, Rex," said Libby. "I think your day has been, too. I'll untie you and let you run free. That should make you happy." Libby unhooked the chain from his collar. Rex barked and ran and leaped around Libby. She had made Goosy Poosy and Rex happy. Who would make her happy?

"Libby?" Vera stood at the back door, motioning for Libby.

Libby ran to her with Rex beside her and Goosy Poosy honking and running behind her. Libby thought Vera looked very pretty in her yellow dress.

"Libby, Susan told me about the strange party." Vera slipped her arm around Libby's thin shoulders. "I'm very sorry something like this happened. Don't let it discourage you. You have another one Monday. I'm sure it will be just as nice as Jason's party."

"I wish everything would go just right all the time." Libby sighed. "I don't like things to go wrong."

Vera hugged Libby, then released her. "Susan said she got a letter from Mark McCall. It was very nice of him to write."

Libby turned away, her hand on Rex's head. He stood close to her and she felt better.

"Susan also told me about Brian Parr's ring."

Libby quickly pulled it out of her pocket. As Vera looked at the ring Libby told her where she'd found it, then about the Rouches' strange behavior.

"I think we should take this to Lisa. I can't imagine how it got on our back field." Vera frowned thoughtfully and studied the ring as if it would tell her something. She shrugged. "Maybe I'm making too much of it. Brian might have lost it a few weeks ago when he was helping hay."

"Should I take it to show Lisa right now?" Libby took the ring from Vera. Something about finding the ring kept nagging at the back of her mind. What was she trying to remember?

"I'll call Susan to go with you." Vera hurried into the house, calling Susan.

Libby didn't want to talk to Susan. She would be full of the letter from Mark. Libby did not want to hear anything Mark wrote to Susan. What if Susan offered to let her read it? That would be terrible!

But Susan didn't say anything about the letter. She rode her bike beside Libby all the way to Lisa's house and didn't say a word! Libby was ready to burst. She noticed Susan's extra red cheeks. What had Mark said? Twice Libby started to ask, then bit her lower lip to keep her big mouth shut. She would not ask! If Susan wanted to tell her, she would. Oh, but it was hard not to ask!

"Do you have the ring?" asked Susan as they knocked at Lisa's door.

"Of course." Libby frowned at Susan. Did Susan think she was dumb?

Lisa opened the door and invited them in. It was cool and comfortable inside the small house. The curtains were closed to block out the hot sun.

"Amy is down for her nap," said Lisa as she sat on the floor in front of the sofa. Susan and Libby sat across from her on the floor. "Amy will be sorry she missed your visit. She loves both of you." Lisa smiled at the girls.

Libby pulled the ring out and held it out to Lisa. Before she could say a word Lisa grabbed it with a loud exclamation.

"This is Brian's ring. He never, never took it off." Lisa closed her hand over the ring and pressed it to her heart. Tears stood in her eyes, then slowly ran down her suddenly pale cheeks. "Where did you get it?"

Suddenly Libby was scared to tell Lisa. Finding Brian's ring was not good news at all!

"Tell her, Libby," said Susan sharply.

Libby began slowly. "It was in the pasture in back of the barn where we keep the yearlings." She saw the fear leap in Lisa's eyes. "It doesn't mean anything, Lisa. Mom said maybe he dropped it when he helped with the haying."

"No! No, he had it after that." She shook her head in agony. "I know something terrible happened to him. I know he wouldn't just walk out on us. Oh, he's hurt or dead or something awful!"

Libby didn't know what to do. She wanted to say something that would make Lisa feel better. What could she say? Her tongue seemed too big for her mouth. A hard lump settled in her throat.

Susan awkwardly patted Lisa's shoulder. "Brian has to be all right. We prayed. Remember?"

Lisa nodded as she wiped away her tears. "We did! And I believe that God is answering. Brian will come home safe!" Lisa looked at Libby. "Tell me again right where you found the ring? Was anything else of his there?"

Once again Libby told about the ring.

"You mean you just stumbled over a stick and the ring just lay in the weeds?" asked Lisa, frowning. "How could you find the ring like that? The ring is not big enough for you to see easily."

Suddenly Libby remembered what had bothered her before about finding the ring. She leaned forward, her cheeks flushed, her hazel eyes wide. "That was the strange part. I just remembered. The ring was around a stick and the stick was poked into the ground. That was what I tripped over."

Lisa jumped to her feet. "Was that all that was there? Maybe there was something else and you missed it."

Libby frowned thoughtfully. "Maybe. I could go look again. I'm sure I could find the spot again."

Lisa turned to Susan. "Will you stay here with

63

Amy while I go with Libby? We'll be back as soon as possible. I must find out what else is there!"

"I'll stay," said Susan quickly. "I'll call Mom and tell her what we're doing. If Amy wakes up, I can take good care of her."

Lisa's face was flushed and her movements jerky as she pulled on tennis shoes and tied them. She explained to Susan about Amy's food in the refrigerator and her diapers. "Can I use your bike, Susan?"

Susan nodded and Libby and Lisa hurried outdoors. Libby was beginning to feel Lisa's urgency. What if she had overlooked something?

Libby showed Lisa the shortcut on the road back of the Johnson farm. Just as they reached the corner of the Johnson property Libby saw a small dark blue car pull away from the side of the road. Inside the car sat Pete, Lorraine, and Gary Rousch. They saw her and acted very angry. Had they been trespassing again? What were they after?

"Hurry, Elizabeth," said Lisa, looking over her shoulder at Libby. "I must see where you found Brian's ring."

Libby crawled through the fence, then held it up for Lisa to cross. Grass lay trampled down as if someone else had crawled through the same spot, and often. Had it been the Rousch family?

Quickly Libby found the spot where she'd found the ring. Frantically she looked around. Was it the spot? Why did it look so different?

"Why would anyone rake around these trees?" asked Lisa in surprise.

Libby gasped. That's what looked different. She could not find where she'd stood or where the ring had been. Finally she gave up. "Maybe Ben can. He was with me. He might have noticed more than I did."

Tears spilled down Lisa's flushed cheeks. A deer fly buzzed around her head and she swatted it impatiently away. "I have to know! We'll get Ben!"

"Let's look around one more time," said Libby. She knew Ben was bike riding with Brenda. She had no idea when he'd be home.

Finally they gave up. Libby felt too hot to move. Lisa was breathing hard as she leaned against a tree to catch her breath. She'd scattered leaves and dried brush and weeds as she'd frantically looked.

"I'll get Ben out here," said Lisa. "He'll know. Won't he, Libby? He will find the spot!"

He probably would, but what good would it do? If there had been anything else that belonged to Brian they would have found it. Ben couldn't find something that wasn't there.

Lisa walked to the fence with drooping shoulders. "We might as well go back. I'm sure Amy's awake by now."

Libby felt like crying as they pedaled back to Lisa's house. Poor Lisa! Why didn't Brian come home where he belonged?

Susan was walking Amy around the small yard

when they rode in. Amy gurgled and laughed. Lisa hugged her close as she told Libby to send Ben down right away. Libby explained about Ben riding with Brenda, but she would tell him as soon as he came home. Libby told Lisa she would come back with him so she could watch Amy while Lisa and Ben rode to the spot to hunt.

As they rode home Libby told Susan about the Rousch family being near their property again and about finding piles of raked up weeds and grass and branches. "I think we'll have to tell Dad so he can stop them. I wonder what they are looking for."

Susan shrugged. "Maybe they buried something there."

"I heard them say something about a paper. Whatever they want, it's on paper. Could it be a map to a hidden treasure? Or what?"

"I'm sure I don't know." Susan stood on her bike and pedaled quickly away.

Libby stared after her thoughtfully. Susan was certainly acting strangely. Had Mark said something in his letter that upset her?

Eight
Jack and Dan

Libby stared at the mailbox. Would Mark ever write to her? She had mailed a letter to him that she'd written last night. Libby touched the silver mailbox. Also inside was a letter she'd written to her real grandma. Would Grandma LaDere ever write to her? Would she ever love her?

Slowly Libby walked back up the long driveway. Soon it would be time for the birthday party for Tammy Hayes. Ten children were coming. Libby stopped. What if Tammy's birthday turned out like Gary's had? No! It would not! Today's party would be just as much fun as Jason's had been.

"Everything will be fine," said Libby as she continued walking. It would be even better if Susan would stop acting so strangely. Yesterday Susan would not talk to Libby. Even during Sunday school and church Susan had kept away from Libby. What was bothering Susan?

A tractor drove past and blocked out the noise of the farm animals. Libby watched Ben, Kevin, and Toby working in the garden. Ben and Lisa had ridden back to the pasture and looked around again to see if Lisa could find anything else belonging to Brian. With tears in her eyes Lisa had told Libby that they'd found nothing.

Chuck had ridden Tessy to the area and looked around. He had called the police about trespassers and they'd agreed to drive the back road at regular intervals.

Libby had told Chuck about finding Brian's ring and he had told the police. Maybe they would find Brian.

With a sigh Libby walked to the horse pen and watched Rhonda work with Snowball. Rhonda lifted her hand to Libby and said hi. Libby could barely answer. How she wanted to be the one working with Snowball! Libby leaned against the fence. Snowball recognized her and tried to pull away from Rhonda. She kept a firm hold and commanded Snowball to obey her. Libby pressed her lips tightly closed. Her heart raced. Rhonda was not good for Snowball!

Rhonda's blonde hair flew back as she ran with Snowball. Why didn't Rhonda go home where she belonged? Vera had finally called her brother and told him Rhonda was there and why. He had said she should stay a while to think things out. How long did she have to think? Why didn't her parents patch up their quarrel and get back together? Rhonda was ruining Libby's summer!

Libby ducked her head guiltily. She was very selfish! Chuck had said that it was important to think of others. She was not thinking of Rhonda and how she felt. Often Rhonda sat with Vera, crying and hurt. Rhonda wanted her parents to stay together and love each other and be a family again.

Abruptly Libby walked away from the horse pen. She would not think about Rhonda.

Rex ran to Libby, barking happily. Libby rested her hand on Rex's head as she walked to the house. She felt better with Rex beside her.

Susan opened the door just as Libby reached for it. Libby smiled but Susan frowned and walked right past, then ran to the horse pen to be with Rhonda. Libby blinked back tears. Didn't Susan want her for a sister now? What had she done to make Susan stop loving her?

Libby leaned weakly against the back door, tears burning her eyes. She tried to think of something that she'd said or done to Susan, but she couldn't think of anything. But maybe it was the birthday parties! How could that be? Susan had been very happy helping with Jason's party. Something was bothering Susan. Libby pressed her hand against her hot forehead. She had to learn what was wrong with Susan. But right now she had too many things to finish up before Tammy's party.

Libby noticed that Susan kept away from her during and after lunch when they should have worked together to carry the treats and prizes outdoors.

A gentle breeze blew against Libby as she placed the last item on the picnic table. Today was not too hot and not too cool. Libby lifted her face to the breeze and let it blow her damp hair back. Goosy Poosy honked indignantly from the chicken pen. Libby was glad Kevin had remembered to lock up the goose. The children had fun looking at Goosy Poosy. He always showed off for them.

With a frown Libby looked around for Susan. Was she helping Kevin and Toby saddle the horses? Today they would saddle all five horses and let the children ride for a long time. After they rode horses, they'd all climb in the big farm wagon and have Jack and Dan pull them to the back of the farm where they'd have a treasure hunt.

"Elizabeth!"

Libby jerked around at Ben's call. Her heart dropped to her feet at the wild look on his face. "What's wrong?"

"Jack and Dan are gone!" Ben's chest heaved up and down. His face was almost as red as his hair. "The fence is cut and they are gone!"

Libby's hand fluttered at her throat. She could barely breathe. Who would cut the fence?

Ben pushed past Libby and ran into the house, calling his mother. With a pale face Libby

70

followed. This was serious! Jack and Dan were valuable draft horses, a matched gray pair. Chuck loved them. Libby stopped. The plans for the birthday party would be ruined!

Brenda Wilkens had done a lot of mean things since Libby had come to live with the Johnsons. Maybe Brenda wanted to stop the birthday parties so Libby and Susan couldn't help Lisa and baby Amy. Libby gasped at the thought. Even Brenda would not do that, would she?

Libby listened anxiously as Vera called Chuck and told him what was happening. When Vera hung up the receiver, she turned to Libby and Ben with a pale face.

"Dad said to go look for them, Ben. I'll call around the neighborhood to see if anyone knows where they are. Libby, you'll have guests soon. You and Susan will have to have the party right here. Just change a few of your plans. Can you handle that?"

Libby nodded. She could not talk around the lump in her throat. How could she rearrange the party? Just this morning she had taken the "treasures" back near Ben's Christmas trees and hidden them. What could they use for prizes?

The grandfather clock bonged one and Libby dashed from the house. The guests might already be outdoors. Chuck had said that God was concerned about every situation in Libby's life. Chuck had said that God loved her so much that he wanted what was best for her, that he would help her always. Right now she needed help badly. As Libby ran to the horse pen for Susan she asked her heavenly Father for help. How wonderful to know God cared enough to help her!

"Here comes a car," said Susan breathlessly. "Oh, Libby! Ben must find Jack and Dan!"

"I'll help you girls," said Rhonda, neatly tucking her blue plaid shirt into her jeans. "Tell me what to do, and I'll do it."

Libby stared in surprise. She didn't know Rhonda could be nice. "You can help Kevin and Toby line the horses up to ride, Rhonda." Libby smiled and was surprised how easy it was. "Thanks."

Rhonda shrugged, then smiled. "I'm good with organizing games, too."

"You might have to," said Susan with a flip of her red-gold pony tails. "Let's go meet the birthday girl, Libby."

Libby stared at Susan for a second before she walked to the van full of children. Susan had sounded as if she'd had to force herself to talk to her. Oh, what was bothering Susan? The problem would have to be put aside for now.

With a bright smile Libby introduced herself and Susan, then welcomed the birthday girl and the other children. Libby led them directly to the horse pen where they would take turns riding. Five rode at once and the other five chose to watch instead of playing a game. Libby was glad of that. None of the children had ridden before, so Libby was very thankful for Rhonda's help.

Proudly Libby looked at Tessy, Apache Girl, Star, Dusty, and Sleepy. They were all well-mannered—even Sleepy, who had only been on the farm since Toby had been adopted in May. How awful it would be if one of the horses or ponies tried to nip the children. Suddenly Libby stopped mid-thought. Snowball nipped often. Libby had not tried to stop her. Snowball would not obey at all. Libby smiled. Chuck had allowed Rhonda to train Snowball into the best filly possible. Libby could not have done that. Libby nodded. Rhonda was doing what *she* couldn't do. Someday Snowball would be as well-mannered and as well-trained as the horses here in the pen. Someday Snowball could be as trustworthy as the horses that the children were riding.

Libby glanced at Rhonda beside Tessy. Just as soon as possible she would apologize to Rhonda. And she would try to make her visit more enjoyable.

First turns were over and the five children dismounted reluctantly. Libby looked toward the fence to call the other five, then stopped. There were six kids standing at the fence. The sixth was Gary Rousch!

Libby closed her eyes tightly, then looked again. It *was* Gary. Had he been in the van and she not noticed? Was he a friend of Tammy Hayes? He was older than the others, but he could have been invited. Dare she ask Mrs. Hayes?

"Sleepy is having fun, Libby," said Toby with a wide smile.

"He sure is," said Libby. She was very glad for Toby and Kevin's help. Both boys knew several of the children from school. It made it easier to get acquainted.

Just as the rides were finished, Ben walked into the yard leading Jack and Dan.

Libby almost shouted with happiness. Now the children could go on the wagon ride. While Ben harnessed the team, she would show the children all the animals around the farm. Some of them had never seen real sheep. None of them had ever touched a live Goosy Poosy.

Later while Rhonda and Susan led the kids in a game of follow-the-leader, Libby hurried to help Ben.

"Where did you find Jack and Dan?" Libby locked her fingers together and waited. She could tell by Ben's face that he was very excited.

Nervously Ben pushed his red hair off his wide forehead. He licked his lips. "You'll never believe this."

"What? What, Ben?" Libby could barely stand still.

"Jack and Dan were tied up in a grove of trees near Lisa's house. Tied up! I looked around but nobody was there with them. I just untied them and brought them home."

"Did you tell Mom?"

Ben nodded. A cat rubbed against his leg but

he ignored it. "She went in the house to call Dad."

"Jack and Dan weren't hurt, were they?" Libby rubbed her hands down Dan's shiny gray coat. She couldn't stand it if they were hurt.

"Not hurt at all," said Ben with a puzzled frown. "I can't understand why anyone would cut the fence, then take the horses such a short way. Maybe whoever took the horses to the trees thought someone would be there with a truck." Ben shook his head. "I don't understand it."

Maybe Brenda Wilkens had done it. She would do something like that just to cause trouble. Libby opened her mouth to say it, then closed it. Ben could get mad if she suggested that Brenda had done it. Joe might know. He would tell the truth. Later she would call him and ask him.

Ben led Jack and Dan into the driveway, then waited as Susan and Rhonda helped the children into the wagon. Libby counted them. Ten. She counted again. Ten! Her heart zoomed to her feet. Had they lost someone? She looked at the children again. Gary Rousch was not there!

Libby forced herself to remain calm as she talked to Mrs. Hayes.

"I didn't invite Gary Rousch," said Mrs. Hayes as she shook her head. "I don't know the boy."

Weakly Libby climbed into the wagon and motioned for Ben to drive. Why had Gary Rousch been at the party earlier? Where did he go?

Nine
Buried treasures

Libby leaned against the side of the swaying wagon. She must not think about Gary Rousch! The laughing and talking and singing children in the wagon needed her attention. Susan was not any help at all. She sat in the back corner of the wagon just staring off into space. Rhonda was telling a story to the children next to her. Libby couldn't hear what she was saying, but by the children's expressions, it was interesting and funny. Rhonda really was helping! Susan might as well have stayed home.

Ben turned, caught Libby's eye, and motioned for her to come close. She leaned her head near him.

"I just saw someone moving in the trees over there. I'm going to drive closer and check it out."

Libby agreed and leaned back in place. Would the Rousch family dare come again on their property? What could Ben do if they were there?

A big ugly turkey vulture circled above them, then flew away. The children shouted after it, asking what was dead. Susan answered them, then sat back in her corner, her face set. Libby wanted to ask Susan what was bothering her, but she couldn't in front of the children.

As Ben reached the trees Libby sat up straight and peered ahead, her eyes narrowed. Was someone moving around among the trees? Maybe her imagination was working hard. She leaned up to Ben. "Did you see anything?" she asked anxiously.

Ben shook his head and turned the team back where they'd planned on going.

"Go faster!" shouted one of the boys.

Ben turned his head with a grin. "Hang on tight and I will."

"Not too fast," warned Mrs. Hayes.

Libby laughed along with the children as the wagon swayed and rattled across the pasture. Soon they would reach the Christmas trees where she had buried the treasures for the children to find. She patted her pocket where she'd slipped the treasure maps that Chuck and Ben had drawn the night before.

"This is just like old times," Chuck had said with a laugh as he drew the maps. "When I was a boy I loved to hide a treasure, then draw a map and find it." He had chuckled and seemed almost as young as Ben. "And I never missed. I found the treasure every time."

Finally Ben pulled Jack and Dan to a stop and

the children scrambled from the wagon. Libby called for them to stand in a line next to the wagon while she gave them the rules of the game and the maps. She laughed at their excitement.

"Libby, look!" Susan pointed toward a large blue spruce.

Libby gasped. The treasure she'd buried under the blue spruce was lying on top of the ground with a pile of dirt beside it. Wildly she looked around to the places where she had hidden the treasures. The ones within view were sitting out on the ground. Who had done that? The person had to have watched her hide them to know where they were. Brenda? If so, why? Libby looked helplessly at Susan, then Rhonda. Susan looked as if she didn't care.

"I have an idea," said Rhonda, stepping forward. "Kids, each of you take the map you have and follow it anyway just to see if you can. After you get your gift, take it to the wagon, and then we'll play hide and seek among the trees."

Libby leaned weakly against the wagon as Rhonda organized everything. Ben tried to comfort her but she brushed him aside. She did not want anyone talking to her or looking at her. Why didn't anything she did turn out right?

"Stop feeling sorry for yourself," snapped Susan.

Libby lifted her head, her pointed chin out, her eyes flashing. "Mind your own business!"

"This is my business. We are in this together. It's not your fault that some ornery person dug up the treasures." Susan stood with her feet apart, her hands on her hips. "I think someone is trying to ruin our birthday party business. I don't think Mrs. Wilkens would do any of this, but I'm sure Brenda would. We will talk to her after everyone leaves. We'll make her tell the truth."

"Ben will get mad."

Susan shrugged. "So?"

Libby smiled. "I'm glad you're not mad at me anymore, Susan. I don't know what I did to you, but I am sorry. I love you."

Susan turned away, her head down.

Libby groaned. Susan did hate her! A cold knot settled in Libby's stomach and she wanted to sink down on the ground and sob. Libby noticed Susan's shoulders shaking. Why, Susan was crying! "You don't have to cry, Susan. I know you can't help it if you hate me. I'm ugly and mean and can't do anything right." Scalding tears slipped down Libby's face and she was glad Ben was with the children playing hide and seek.

"Oh, Libby!" Susan touched Libby's arm. "I don't hate you. I love you. You're my sister!" Susan hung her head and twisted the toe of her tennis shoe in the tall grass. "It's you who should hate me."

Libby's eyes widened. "Why?"

"I . . . I did a terrible thing. I can't stand myself another minute! I feel awful!"

"What did you do, Susan?" She hadn't dug up the treasures, had she?

Susan took a deep breath and looked right at

79

Libby. "You got a letter from Mark McCall."

Libby shook her head. "No, *you* did."

Susan sighed. "I did. But, Libby, you did too, and I tore yours up and burned it! Oh, Libby! I feel terrible. I'm sorry. Please, please forgive me!"

Libby stared speechlessly at Susan. Mark had written her a letter. Susan had ripped it up before she could see it or read it. How could Susan do such a thing?

"Your letter was much nicer than mine and it made me mad." Susan sounded as if she would burst into tears again. "I wanted Mark to write a long letter to me, but he didn't. But your letter was two pages long! Oh, Libby, I'm sorry!"

Susan looked so unhappy that Libby couldn't be mad at her. "I forgive you, Susan. Please tell me everything Mark wrote."

Susan sniffed hard and smiled. "He said that Old Zeb went to church with them last Sunday. And he described how he and Shauna are training Sunlight and Midnight. Holly is going to write to you, too." Susan frowned thoughtfully, then continued until she couldn't remember another thing.

By the time the children raced back to the wagon Libby was happier than she had been in days. She and Susan were friends again. Susan had not been mad at her because she was ugly or mean or anything. She hadn't done anything. Libby smiled happily. Not even the dug-up buried treasures could make her feel bad right now.

Later the children clustered around the picnic table for cake and ice cream and punch. Tammy received wonderful gifts that made her very happy. Libby remembered all her birthdays when she hadn't received any presents and no one had baked her a cake. No one had even remembered to say happy birthday. But that was all past. On her twelfth birthday she'd had a beautiful birthday cake with candles. Her new family had given her Snowball and a saddle, a bridle, and a nice leather halter.

She smiled as she looked across the yard. The smile left her face. Gary Rousch stood at the corner of the house. He jumped back out of sight when he saw Libby look at him. Gary Rousch again! Was he so eager to be at a birthday party that he came just to watch? Had he ever received anything nice for his birthday? Did his mother bake him a cake and stick candles in it?

Libby wanted to find him and talk to him but she was kept busy with the party. She didn't see him again. After the van full of children pulled out of the driveway, she looked again. Gary Rousch was gone. Or he was too well hidden for her to find him.

Rhonda and Vera helped Libby and Susan clean up. As they worked, Libby told about the strange happenings. Chuck drove in just as the last piece of garbage was dropped in the burn barrel. Everyone gathered around him.

"I talked to the police about Jack and Dan," Chuck said as he sank down on the bench beside the picnic table. Kevin and Toby sat beside him.

Susan poured him a tall glass of iced punch and handed it to him. He thanked her with a kiss and a quick hug. Libby stood back and wished she had thought of giving him punch first.

Libby listened as Chuck talked. He asked questions and everyone helped with the answers.

"We seem to have a mystery on our hands." Chuck drummed his fingers on the picnic table. "I don't know what to make of it."

"I think it's Brenda Wilkens again," said Kevin as he pushed his glasses up against his nose.

Ben frowned at him. "You always think everything that goes wrong around here is Brenda's fault."

"You must admit a lot of it is," said Vera. "I don't think we should disregard Brenda. Maybe she is innocent. But maybe she is guilty."

"She'll be sorry if she is!" cried Libby, her eyes flashing. "No matter what she does or what Mrs. Wilkens does, we are going to help Lisa keep Amy."

"Easy, Elizabeth." Chuck reached across the table and patted her arm. "I'll have a talk with her parents and find out what I can." He sighed. "I sure hate to have hard feelings with the Wilkens family, but they seem to want it that way."

"Not Joe," said Susan, nudging Libby.

Libby flushed and looked down at her clenched hands. She knew Joe liked her. She liked him, too.

"Ben, I want you to put all the horses in the barn tonight," said Chuck. "We'll lock it up tight and then leave Goosy Poosy loose for the night. If anyone comes into the yard, we'll know about it."

Toby laughed. "*Everyone* will know about it."

"I could sleep in the barn and keep watch," said Ben eagerly.

"No!" Vera frowned sharply. "You will not do that!"

Chuck took her hand and held it firmly. "That won't be necessary. The police said they will patrol the area tonight. They said we should leave the yard light on all night just to discourage anyone who might want to try something."

Libby shivered. Chuck must not think Brenda did anything. He must think a real burglar or rustler or someone had done everything. Or did he suspect the Rousch family? Libby clasped her hands tightly in her lap. Tomorrow was another party. Would Gary Rousch attend again? Would anything go wrong?

Libby looked at Susan beside her and smiled. No matter what happened, she and Susan were friends again—not just friends, but sisters.

Ten
Brenda

"I have been thinking about Brian's ring," said Lisa Parr. "Elizabeth, tell me again the details of finding it." Lisa sat on the couch with Amy on her lap.

Libby looked quickly at Susan on the floor beside her, then thoughtfully told the story Lisa wanted to hear. Libby felt sorry for Lisa. Dark rings circled her eyes. Today she looked almost as old as Vera. Lisa must not have slept much the past few days.

Libby finished the story and all was quiet except Amy's occasional baby chatter.

Two days ago Chuck had talked to Mr. Wilkens. Susan and Libby had talked to Brenda. To Libby's amazement she believed Brenda when she acted surprised at the strange happenings.

Yesterday had been Megan Brovont's birthday party. Libby sighed. Everything had gone well.

But once again Gary Rousch had been there. Once she'd almost caught him. He'd run away and she hadn't seen him again. Did Gary know that she didn't have a party scheduled for today? Maybe he would come and then they could grab him and hold onto him long enough to find out what he wanted.

Amy dropped her ring of plastic keys and Libby jumped in surprise. She laughed self-consciously.

"Why would Brian take off his ring and drop it on the ground?" Lisa shook her head, her blue eyes narrowed thoughtfully. "I think someone took the ring from him!"

"Why?" asked Susan. She rested her hands on her knees. "Why would anyone want to take Brian's ring? It's only a class ring."

Lisa's shoulders sagged. "You're right. I just don't want to think that he took it off and threw it away so he wouldn't have to think about his past life."

"What about his wedding ring?" Libby looked up hopefully.

"He doesn't have one. I didn't have the money and he said he didn't really mind." Impatiently Lisa pushed herself up. She stood Amy on the floor next to the couch. "I can't think about it anymore. I can see Brian hurt and dying in the woods or in a ditch somewhere." Lisa shook her head hard, her dark hair bouncing around her face. "I won't think about it! Brian is alive and well! He will come home soon! Oh, he must! I miss him so much!" Tears streamed down her cheeks and Libby squirmed uncomfortably.

"Don't cry, Lisa," said Susan softly. "Brian will come home. Wait and see."

Libby jumped up. "Why don't you come to our house today? You can help us get ready for Friday's birthday party." Libby did not like to leave Lisa alone when she was feeling so bad. Libby knew how much it hurt.

"You girls are good friends to me," said Lisa, drying her eyes. "I'm so glad the Lord sent you to me."

Libby smiled. Not long ago no one wanted her. Now several people did. Maybe it would be this way from now on. Could anyone ever be happy forever? Did love last forever?

"I'd like to come help you," said Lisa with a watery smile. "Give me time to get Amy's diaper bag ready and we can go."

Just as Lisa walked into the tiny bedroom someone knocked on the front door. "Get that, girls," she called. "I'll be right there."

Libby opened the door, then gasped in surprise. The short, plump woman standing there with a frown on her round face was Mrs. Blevins from Social Services. Libby had seen her often when she'd been in and out with Miss Miller.

Mrs. Blevins stared at Libby, then shrugged as if she couldn't care less that she couldn't place her. "I came to see Mrs. Parr."

"About what?" Libby stood right in the

woman's way so she couldn't just walk in. Libby's heart raced. Was the woman here to take Amy away?

"Business, and none of it yours," snapped the woman. Suddenly she looked at Libby in recognition. "Elizabeth Gail Dobbs. Now I remember. You look different but your manners are still the same. Let me in. I want to talk to Mrs. Parr."

Libby looked helplessly at Susan, then slowly stepped out of Mrs. Blevins' way.

"Who is it?" asked Lisa, walking from the bedroom with Amy on her hip and the diaper bag in her hand. Lisa stopped suddenly, her face pale.

Mrs. Blevins stepped forward and introduced herself in her usual cold voice and abrupt manner. "I've had a report on you, Mrs. Parr. It's my duty to check it out." She looked around the room and Libby wanted to sink through the floor. Usually Lisa was a very good housekeeper, but today the room was messy.

"When have you and the baby eaten last?" asked Mrs. Blevins coldly.

Lisa squared her shoulders and lifted her chin. "Just at lunch time. When have you? Do you want lunch?"

Mrs. Blevins' face flushed. "I want to see the kitchen. You can't live here with a baby and not have food in the house."

Libby wanted to grab the woman and shove her out the door. "Lisa is coming to our house right now. We have plenty of food at our house."

"Sit down over there and shut up," commanded Mrs. Blevins, pointing to a chair near the window. "I will not put up with your insolence."

"If my dad was here you wouldn't talk to Libby like that," said Susan, locking her fingers together.

"So, Elizabeth Gail Dobbs has taught you a fine lesson in rudeness, has she? Get out of my way. I have business to attend to and I won't allow two little girls to stop me."

Amy whimpered and snuggled close to Lisa.

"Why is that baby crying?" Mrs. Blevins walked close and looked at Amy critically. "Is she hungry or hurt?" She touched a bruise on Amy's leg. "Do you hit her hard enough to bruise her?"

"She fell down yesterday." Lisa sounded as if she would burst into tears any minute. "Amy is fine. She is not hungry or hurt. I take good care of her."

"I'll be the judge of that!"

Libby wanted to punch the woman in the nose. How could she be so mean?

Abruptly the woman walked to the small kitchen and opened cupboard doors and checked the refrigerator. She clicked her tongue several times and mumbled to herself.

By the time she left, Lisa was a nervous wreck. Libby and Susan took her home with them and Vera helped calm her down.

"I wish you would have called me when she walked in the house," said Vera as she put a cup of tea in front of Lisa. "I would have told you to forbid her to look around. You know she was there only because Mrs. Wilkens reported you. Mrs. Blevins and Mrs. Wilkens are friends. Mrs. Blevins could have bluffed her way around your house. She might not have had any authority to do what she did." Vera shook her head. "But she might get the necessary papers to take Amy. It's hard to tell what she'll do. She is a very unhappy woman—and overworked."

"Why doesn't Mrs. Wilkens mind her own business?" asked Lisa, her face pale. "What have I done to her? I can take care of Amy by myself until Brian gets home. But maybe she doesn't think Brian will ever get home."

Vera talked quietly to Lisa until she felt better again.

Libby could not sit still a minute longer. "Susan and I will take Amy outdoors to play. I'll have Kevin lock up Goosy Poosy so he doesn't scare Amy."

"Watch so she doesn't put stones or things in her mouth."

"Who would want to eat stones and sticks and leaves?" asked Susan, making a face.

Vera laughed and tapped Susan on the shoulder. "You did, and I'm sure Libby did, too. Babies like to put things in their mouths."

"We'll watch Amy carefully," promised Libby as she hoisted Amy on her hip.

The sun shone brightly and Libby blinked against the glare of it. She carried Amy to the front yard in the shade of the big trees. Susan took one hand and Libby the other and they walked Amy around the yard. Amy laughed and gurgled. When she grew tired, Libby carried her.

The girls discussed Mrs. Blevins and what Lisa should do. They planned Friday's party. An airplane flew overhead. A car without a muffler drove past. A honey bee buzzed around the roses in the front yard.

Libby looked down at Amy. "Look, Susan."

"She's asleep. We'll take her in the house and lay her on the carpet in the family room."

Several minutes later Libby and Susan walked back outdoors by themselves. They had left Vera, Rhonda, and Lisa talking about God's Word and discussing what some Scriptures meant.

Susan clutched Libby's arm. "Look who's coming," she whispered in surprise. "She had better not be coming to cause trouble."

Libby watched as Brenda Wilkens rode her bike right up to them. Brenda's face was flushed and hot. She was dressed in red shorts and a red and white sun top.

"Is Lisa here?" asked Brenda breathlessly.

"What if she is?" Libby stood with her fists doubled at her sides. She would not take any more trouble from Brenda or her mother.

"I have to talk to her." Brenda twisted her

fingers in agitation. "I have to talk to her right now!"

"What is it, Brenda?" asked Susan in concern. "You seem so upset. What's wrong?"

"Oh, Susan!" Brenda clutched Susan's arm. "Mother is going to have Amy taken away from Lisa."

"She wouldn't dare!" cried Libby.

"But she is! I heard her talking just a few minutes ago to Mrs. Blevins. She is going to take Amy this afternoon! I must warn Lisa!"

Libby blinked in surprise. "You want to help Lisa?"

Brenda frowned. "Of course I do. She's my friend! I don't want Amy taken from her."

"What can we do?" asked Susan tearfully.

Libby narrowed her eyes and cocked her head. "If Lisa is not home, how can Mrs. Blevins take Amy?" Libby laughed in delight. "We will ask Lisa to stay with us for a few days. Mrs. Blevins can't take Amy away if they are staying with us and we're taking care of both of them!"

"That's wonderful, Libby!" cried Brenda with a smile.

Libby almost fainted. Brenda called her Libby. Brenda smiled at her! "Thank you, Brenda, for telling us your mother's plan. I'm glad you did."

"And so am I!" cried Susan.

Brenda suddenly backed away. "I can't stay here all day talking to you girls. I've got important things to do." She flipped her long hair over her slender shoulders and walked to her bike.

Libby stared after her. Brenda could be nice when she wanted to be. What a surprise!

Eleven
Help for Rhonda

Libby helped Chuck set Amy's crib up in the spare room. Rhonda had moved into Susan's room, and Susan in with Libby.

"Just let Mrs. Blevins try to get Amy now," said Susan with her hands on her hips. "Lisa and Amy are safe with us."

Chuck stepped back from the crib. "It's been a long time since we had a crib in this house. It's kind of nice to see one again. Amy won't even know that she's not home."

"Thanks, Dad," said Libby, hugging Chuck warmly. "I'm glad you and Mom agreed to have Lisa and Amy stay here for a while."

"We have the best dad in the whole world," said Susan, hugging him.

"I know that," said Chuck, grinning. "But a very hungry dad. Let's go eat supper. I smelled fried chicken."

"Lisa baked a cake and Rhonda made a big

tossed salad." Susan walked downstairs with her arm through Chuck's.

Libby walked behind them, wishing she was in Susan's place.

Susan chatted on and on and Libby wanted to tell her to keep quiet a while and give someone else a chance to talk. It had been a long time since she'd spent an hour in Chuck's study just talking to him, listening to his advice and wisdom. She missed those times. How would it feel to be the only child? That way she'd have him all to herself when she wanted. But that wouldn't be good either. She liked talking with Ben and Susan, playing games with Kevin and Toby. She would not complain. She had a wonderful family.

Rhonda walked from the family room. Poor Rhonda! She did not have a happy family. Did she spend time talking to her parents?

"Uncle Chuck, I have to talk to you." Tears were in Rhonda's blue eyes. She twisted her fingers nervously.

"Sure, honey." Chuck slipped his arm around her slender shoulders. "Come in the study and we'll talk." He looked at Susan. "Tell Mom to go ahead with dinner. We'll be there in a few minutes."

Libby watched them go with a strange feeling around her heart. At first she had hated the talks with Chuck. Going into the study to talk had always meant that once again she was in trouble.

But not anymore. Would Chuck ever find time to talk to her again?

Amy made Libby laugh at the supper table so she felt better. It was fun watching a baby eat.

Chuck and Rhonda walked in while everyone was laughing. Vera explained what was funny. Libby studied Rhonda. She looked a little happier. Chuck always knew just the right thing to say. And he would have prayed with her. Chuck always said that praying together, agreeing together for an answer was very important. He knew God would answer.

It seemed to Libby that for the rest of the evening Rhonda took Chuck's attention. Libby could not talk to him. When she started, Rhonda would butt in and he would talk to her. Libby wanted to pull Rhonda's long blonde hair out at the roots!

Finally Libby gave up and walked to the kitchen. She might as well spend her time alone in the kitchen with a glass of orange juice. Chuck didn't have time for her. Rhonda made sure of that.

Slowly Libby sipped her juice. She stared out the kitchen window. It stayed light out until almost ten o'clock during the summer. She liked playing outdoors with the others at night. Joe walked down often to play tag or hide and seek. Brenda only came when they were going to play indoor games.

Libby turned at a sound behind her. It was

Rhonda. Libby turned back to stare out the window. She would not talk to Rhonda. And Rhonda had better not say anything to her!

"Waiting for your boyfriend?" asked Rhonda as she filled a glass with cold water.

Libby took a deep breath and closed her eyes. She would not answer!

"Why are you mad at me?" asked Rhonda. "What have I done to you?"

Libby spun around, her eyes flashing. "Go home where you belong! I don't want you here!"

Rhonda backed against the sink, her face white.

"Your parents will never get back together! You'll end up in a foster home where nobody will like you." Libby tried to stop the words but they were out before she could. How could she be so mean to Rhonda?

"I hate you, Elizabeth Gail Dobbs! I hope you're never adopted!"

Libby's legs gave way and she sank to a chair. The glass fell to the floor, splattering juice around.

"Look what you did! What a dumb girl you are, Libby."

Tears filled Libby's eyes. "I *will* be adopted," she said woodenly. "My name will be Elizabeth Gail Johnson."

Rhonda dropped to the floor beside Libby. "I'm sorry. Forgive me, please. I was angry."

Libby sniffed hard. "I don't want your parents to split up, Rhonda. I shouldn't have said that. I want you to be happy. I want them to be happy together."

"Oh, so do I!"

"Did you tell them how you feel?"

Rhonda slowly stood up and pressed her hands together in front of her. "I tried, but I got so upset that I couldn't. I just ran."

"Running away never helps anything, Rhonda." Libby suddenly felt about fifty years old. Others had told her how important it was to stay to face your troubles. "It's better to stay and take care of the problems."

Rhonda squared her shoulders. "Uncle Chuck said the same thing to me. I didn't want to do it, but I think I will. Mom and Dad must listen to me. I belong to them. They'll want to hear what I have to say."

"Sure they will." Libby managed a smile. "Why don't you call your dad right now and tell him you're coming home."

Rhonda hesitated. "It's harder to do than it seems. I . . . I don't think I can."

"Yes, you can." Libby lifted the receiver and handed it to Rhonda.

"Stay here with me. I'm afraid." Rhonda's hand trembled as she took the phone, then dialed.

Libby sat beside Rhonda, reassuring her that everything would be fine.

"Daddy? It's me." Tears slipped down Rhonda's cheeks. "I'm ready to come home, Daddy. But can we talk? Me and you and Mom?"

She waited, her eyes wide. "OK, Daddy. See you later."

Libby wanted to say something to make Rhonda feel better but she didn't have the words. Why did bad words spill out of her mouth before she could stop them, but good words couldn't be forced out? She'd asked Chuck once and he had said that as she learned to be more and more like Jesus the words would change. Would she ever be like Jesus? Sometimes it seemed impossible! Chuck had said that was why reading the Bible was important. He said that the Bible gave a true picture of Jesus. Only as each person saw Jesus as he is, would he learn to live like him and be like him.

Rhonda hugged Libby, then stood back, her face shining. "Daddy and Mom are coming tonight to pick me up. They both promised to talk to me and to talk to Uncle Chuck and Aunt Vera. Daddy said together we'd find the right answer."

"I'm glad!" Libby's eyes sparkled. "Let's go tell the others."

Libby watched as Rhonda told her news. Vera was the happiest.

"I know my brother will do the right thing. But I think it would be very good if we'd all pray for him as well as for Ellen and Rhonda. Divorce is not the answer. Jesus is the answer. He always is, and always will be."

Lisa looked around, then shook her head. "I have never seen a family like this. You are full of love, full of Jesus. I want my family to be just like this. When Brian comes home we will take time together to read the Bible and pray. I can see that you do more than that, Chuck. You practice what the Bible says. I believe that's the secret."

"You're right, Lisa." Chuck shook his head. "We're still learning to put God's Word into practice, but we are trying. Reading the Bible is not enough. Read and then obey. That's what it takes."

"I won't forget that, Uncle Chuck." Rhonda sat on the floor at Chuck's feet.

Libby smiled happily. Let Rhonda sit by Chuck. Libby could sit by him after Rhonda left.

Chuck prayed, then thanked God for the answer. And Libby knew God would answer. He loved them, all of them!

Libby tried to stay awake so she could meet Uncle Steve, Vera's brother, and Aunt Ellen. Finally Libby gave up and sleepily stumbled upstairs. Susan was already asleep in her bed. Libby slipped on her yellow nightgown and climbed into bed. Susan turned over and mumbled in her sleep. Libby turned so the cool breeze from the open window blew on her. Once she heard Rex bark, then nothing more.

Suddenly Libby awoke with a start. How long had she slept? What had awakened her? Moonlight flooded the room. Libby sat up. Had Rhonda's parents come for her? Libby could not wait until morning to find out.

Slowly Libby walked to Susan's room. She

peeked in. The bed was still made. It hadn't been slept in. Had Rhonda gone home already?

Loud snores came from Toby's room. How could anyone sleep with that noise? Was Toby sucking his thumb while he snored?

Libby stopped at the top of the stairs. Someone was walking up. She gasped, then recognized Chuck. "Hi, Dad," she said softly.

"Elizabeth, you should be asleep. You probably want to know what happened." Chuck slipped his arm around Libby and walked toward her room. "We talked and talked. I showed them that they didn't have to fight this problem themselves, that they had Jesus to help them."

Libby's heart leaped. It was working out great for Rhonda!

"Rhonda told them how she feels and they told how they feel. I think that was the first time they really got things in the open. Elizabeth, it's so important to express your feelings. Never, never let them build up like Steve, Ellen, and Rhonda did. Talk things out always."

"And are they going to stay together?"

"Yes. They had decided to for Rhonda's sake, but after we talked they knew there was hope for both of them. Steve and Ellen both asked Jesus to teach them love." Chuck squeezed Libby. "And he will."

"I love you, Dad."

"I love you, Elizabeth. I've missed our talks. I will be glad when we aren't this busy."

Libby kissed Chuck, then walked happily to

bed. She felt like singing and shouting and dancing. He still loved her. He still enjoyed talking with her.

Libby climbed into bed beside Susan, then smiled and closed her eyes.

Twelve
Gary's secret

"Do you think it'll work, Ben?" asked Libby anxiously as she walked toward the picnic table with Ben. "I must catch Gary Rousch and learn why he keeps hanging around our birthday parties."

"Don't worry. I'll catch him, Elizabeth." Ben nodded grimly. "I think Gary Rousch can answer some of our questions. If he shows up again today, I'll catch him for sure."

Libby heaved a sigh of relief. "He's been to four birthday parties so far and no one invited him. He is very strange."

Soon Libby was so busy with the party that she didn't have time to worry about Gary Rousch. Today fifteen children, all about nine years old, were celebrating Bobby Adams' ninth birthday. Mr. Adams was coming and he'd asked for a nature hike. Lisa had agreed to take charge of it if Vera would watch Amy.

102

Several times during the party Libby glanced at Ben. He'd shrug to let her know he hadn't seen Gary yet. Maybe Gary wouldn't come today. Or maybe he was staying very well hidden. Libby shivered. It felt terrible knowing someone was watching her for some strange reason. Gary Rousch hadn't been sent by her new case worker, had he? Libby shook her head hard. That was a dumb idea. Miss Kremeen would not use a boy to do her work.

Just as the van was loaded with children and Bobby Adams was shouting thank you and good-bye, Libby caught a glimpse of Gary Rousch beside the chicken coop. Where was Ben? Why wasn't he watching for Gary? Maybe Ben had decided it was too late and Gary wouldn't come.

"Susan. Susan!" whispered Libby frantically. Wouldn't Susan ever hear her? "Susan!"

Susan turned with a frown. "What?" Her voice sounded too loud.

Libby wanted to sink through the ground. "I'm going after Gary Rousch. Tell Ben." Libby dashed toward the chicken house. Gary was already out of sight. She must catch him this time!

The sun felt hotter as Libby ran. Gary Rousch was just disappearing among the trees in back of the chicken house. Did he know that he'd have to run up a hill to get away from her? The sliding hill was between Gary and his freedom. But maybe he could run up a hill as fast as he could run on flat ground.

Libby's side ached and it was hard to catch her breath. A tree branch caught at her hair and she cried out in pain. Had she lost Gary? Oh, where was Ben?

Slower and slower she ran until she thought she'd drop. If she had Star or Apache Girl she wouldn't have any trouble at all. She must catch Gary. She had to know why he kept hanging around.

A flash of a light blue shirt caught her eye. Gary was not far ahead. She could catch him if she tried harder. With a fresh burst of energy Libby ran toward Gary Rousch. Ben would have caught him by now. Ben could run fast and never get tired.

Finally Gary was in plain sight. He turned to look back, tripped, and sprawled headlong in the tall grass. Libby shouted as she forced more speed from her already tired legs. Just as Gary pushed himself up and started running again Libby leaped and tackled him around the legs. He landed with a thud and lay still. Libby clung to him, breathing hard. She would not let go!

"Let me go! You can't keep me here. I'll tell on you!"

Libby's thin chest heaved up and down. "Why have you been spying on us?"

Gary lifted his head and glared at her. "I just wanted to see your birthday parties."

"Elizabeth! I'm coming!" It was Ben racing

toward Libby, his red hair blowing in the breeze. Libby sagged in relief. Now they would get some answers from Gary Rousch.

Ben dragged Gary to his feet. "You are coming back to the house with me. My dad will want to talk to you."

"No!" Gary struggled and almost broke away but Ben kept a tight hold. "I won't talk to anyone!"

Libby saw the fear in Gary's eyes. His face turned a sickly gray. He did know something he wasn't supposed to tell. Was it his secret or his parents'?

"You can talk to us, Gary," said Libby, walking along beside Ben and the frightened Gary. "Tell us why you've been hanging around. If we don't have to tell Dad, we won't. But you tell us or we'll call Dad and the police. Do you want that, Gary Rousch?"

Gary stopped abruptly and Ben almost tumbled over. "My name is not Rousch! Pete is not my dad. He lives with my mother but he is not my dad! I hate him!"

Libby glanced quickly at Ben. Did he know there were homes like that? Probably he would be shocked. "Tell us why you've been sneaking around here," said Libby sharply.

"I can't tell! He'll kill me!"

Ben shook Gary until his hair bounced. "The beating he'll give you won't be anything compared to what the police will do to you."

"Easy, Ben," said Libby, grabbing his arm. "I

think Gary means Pete Rousch will really kill him."

Ben's eyes widened.

"Pete sent me here to keep watch on everyone. He and Mother wanted a chance to find something of theirs that someone hid on your property."

"Why didn't they just ask Dad to let them look?" asked Ben with a scowl. "Dad wouldn't mind. But he doesn't like trespassers."

"Pete couldn't ask." Gary hung his head. "I didn't want to come here. Pete made me. When he saw the ad in the paper about the birthday parties, he said we could come for a party and look around again."

"Look for what, Gary?" Libby stood in front of him, her fists doubled at her sides. "You had better tell us or you'll be in bad trouble."

Gary looked around nervously. "Can't we find shelter? I don't want Pete seeing me talking to you two."

A nervous chill ran down Libby's spine. She looked quickly around. Was Pete watching them right now? Libby hurried beside Ben and Gary to the shelter of the trees in back of the chicken house. Wearily Libby sank to the ground under a large tree with Ben and Gary beside her. "Start talking, Gary. Don't try to lie."

Gary stared from Libby to Ben. "You gotta promise me that you won't ever tell Mother or Pete that I talked to you."

"What if they find out?" asked Libby, her stomach knotting at the answer she knew Gary would give. His mother was a lot like Libby's real mother. And Pete was worse than any of the men who had lived with Mother. Gary was sure in trouble, a lot of trouble!

Gary nervously pushed his hair off his damp forehead. "They can't find out."

"Can't you let us help you, Gary?" Libby felt very sorry for him. "If we can tell Dad he will help find you a good home to live in. You'll be away from your mother and Pete."

Gary shook his head. "Nothing that good would ever happen to me. I tried to run away. Mother gets money for taking care of me. She won't give up that money. And Pete says I help pass them both off as respectable."

"You're making all this up, aren't you?" snapped Ben impatiently. "You talk like a TV program. You can't be talking about real people."

"I believe him, Ben." Libby touched his hand. "Gary does need our help. I think we should help him."

"All right." Ben sighed. "I just hope we're doing the right thing." He frowned at Gary. "Tell us the truth. We'll help you all we can."

Gary took a deep breath. "Remember the warehouse fire two weeks ago? Pete and Mother were paid to burn it down so the owner could collect the insurance. While they were starting the fire, then watching until it had caught, a man happened to be around. He took pictures of them, then tried to get money from them to keep the pictures away from the police."

Libby rubbed her damp palms down her jeans. She could tell that Ben wasn't convinced that Gary was telling the truth. Libby felt he was.

"The man agreed to meet Pete on the back road behind your farm to exchange the negatives for money. I don't know how much. Pete didn't want me to know anything but Mother said she knew I wouldn't tell." Gary shivered even in the heat. "She would make sure I wouldn't tell!" Gary pulled his knees up to his chin and Libby could tell part of the heavy load he was carrying was gone. She knew how good it felt to be able to share troubles with another person who could help.

"Pete drove out to meet the man, then suddenly the man ran away from Pete into your woods. Pete saw him stop long enough to hide something, then run on. Pete almost caught the man, but he got away. We've been trying to find what the man hid. Pete thinks it was the pack of negatives. He thinks the man knew he was going to get caught and he didn't want them on him.

"Who is the man?" asked Ben.

Gary shrugged. "Pete didn't know."

"Why didn't you go to the police with the story?" Ben frowned at Gary as he shifted around.

"I couldn't! Pete would find out. Mother said I couldn't talk about it to anyone!"

108

Libby locked her fingers together and rested her hands in her lap. "You come home with us right now, Gary. Dad will protect you. He will see that you are put in a home where your mother won't be able to find you. But Gary, we must find what the man hid. That will help you."

"No! No, it won't!"

"Why, Gary?" Libby leaned toward him.

"Because I was there! They made me go with them. Pete said since I knew, I'd have to be in on it so I wouldn't break down and tell."

Libby leaped to her feet. "We'll take you to our home. You'll be safe there until Dad can tell the police. Come on!"

Together they ran toward the house. Suddenly Ben stopped, grabbing Gary's arm. "Stay here! Pete Rousch's car is parked in the driveway."

Gary sank to the ground, trembling uncontrollably. "He'll find me. I know he will."

"No, he won't." Libby sat beside Gary and firmly held his hand. "Listen to me. We will stay right here until he drives away. We'll sneak into the house in case he's watching from the road. You are safe, Gary. Safe!"

Tears filled his eyes. "I've never been safe."

"You are now. The Johnson family helped me. They'll help you, too." Libby sat beside Gary until Ben motioned the all clear sign. Chuck would help Gary. Libby just knew he would.

Thirteen
Libby's unusual party

"I don't see how this will help Amy," said Brenda sourly as she stood with the group of boys and girls Libby had called together for a special party.

"We need to find something that's been hidden on our property," explained Libby as patiently as she could. She didn't feel patient. She wanted to load the group in the big farm wagon and have Ben drive them to the spot where Pete had seen the man hide something. But she knew if Brenda didn't understand that by helping them today she was helping baby Amy, then she wouldn't cooperate. "We have had too many things happen that keep us from doing our best with the birthday parties, Brenda. The better the job we do, the more people will want parties, and the more money we'll make for Amy."

"What are we waiting for?" asked Brenda, frowning until her dark brows almost met over her nose.

"Dad is coming with us," said Susan, looking toward the house impatiently. "Oh, I wish he would hurry."

Libby had told Susan what Gary had said. Chuck and Vera knew but they had thought it best not to tell the little boys or Lisa.

Libby sighed as she thought how Gary had looked when Mr. Evans from Social Services had come to pick him up after Chuck's phone call. Mr. Evans had assured all of them that Gary would be carefully placed in a home far enough away that his mother wouldn't find him. But Mr. Evans had said that they'd have to look into the matter to make sure Gary wasn't lying.

The back door opened and Chuck walked out carrying a gallon thermos of iced water that Libby had filled earlier. She had the paper cups already in the wagon. Everyone would get thirsty working in the heat.

"Climb in," shouted Chuck, waving. "We have work to do." He smiled as if he were going on a picnic. Was he thinking of the times he'd gone treasure hunting as a boy?

Libby climbed up beside Joe and Susan. Brenda sat with Ben on the front seat of the wagon. Kevin, Toby, and the friends Libby had called to help sat on the bales of hay that Chuck and Ben had set in the wagon bed.

Talking and laughing filled the air. Libby

smiled. This was more fun than the birthday parties. She caught Susan's eye and lifted her brows. She and Susan shared a secret. They had baked a big cake and used some of their money to buy ice cream and punch. When they drove back to the farm they would have a real party. If they found something, hopefully the negatives, they'd have reason to celebrate. If not, they'd have fun anyway.

Ben stopped Jack and Dan at the edge of the grove of trees. Libby shivered as she thought of what would happen to them if Pete Rousch caught them. The police had promised to patrol the back road regularly. That should keep Pete away.

Libby patted Jack and Dan as she walked past them. Gary had told Chuck how Pete had cut the fence and led Jack and Dan out. He had thought with the horses gone that Ben couldn't drive the wagon on his usual run with the birthday party children. He had meant to take them farther but they had given him trouble. He'd been afraid of them, so he tied them up, hoping that by the time they were found it would be too late for the trip that day. Digging up the treasures had been Gary's idea.

Chuck explained the search pattern he wanted them to follow. Teasing back and forth, they walked the pattern, searching carefully and digging if they thought they should dig.

Once Libby stopped and looked thoughtfully around. Where had she found Brian Parr's ring?

It had to be close to where she was standing. How had his ring come to be here? And around a stick? Libby's eyes widened. Why was Brian's ring around a stick? It wasn't accidentally dropped over that stick. The fit was too tight for that. Why hadn't she thought of that before?

Brian had deliberately pushed his ring onto that stick! Or someone else had. But it had been deliberately done!

Libby looked around for the others. They had all gotten ahead of her. She shrugged. They could look for the negatives or whatever had been hidden. She would try to discover why Brian had left his ring in the woods.

Was this the tree? Libby tilted her head and narrowed her eyes. Was it the tree? She walked close to it, then looked over at the one beside it. Had Ben hidden there?

Slowly Libby walked to another tree, then another. "It has to be one of these."

"Talking to yourself, Elizabeth?" asked Chuck with a grin.

Libby jumped, then shook her head. She was glad to see Chuck. Maybe he could help her puzzle out the riddle. Quickly she told him her thoughts about Brian's ring.

"You didn't tell me about the stick," he said, nodding thoughtfully. "I think you have something. We really shouldn't take time to look around for any clues leading to Brian Parr, but for Lisa's sake I think we will."

With his spade Chuck dug under the three

trees that Libby wasn't sure of. Nothing was turned up.

"It hasn't been dug up around here for a long time," said Chuck, scratching his head. "And if something had been lost on top of the ground, Pete Rousch would have found it. I think we should look somewhere else."

"Where?" Libby could not imagine where else she could look.

"Often as a boy I would hang a treasure in a tree," said Chuck as he looked up. "What branch is low enough for an average-size man to reach?"

Libby could barely stand still as Chuck looked on branches low enough to reach. Shivers ran up and down her spine. She just knew Chuck would find whatever Brian had meant to be found when he'd slipped the ring on that stick.

"Nothing," said Chuck, his shoulders drooping. "Nothing there." He shook his head. "I guess we were wrong, Elizabeth."

"Maybe the others will find something," said Libby hopefully. She didn't want Chuck to be too disappointed.

"Elizabeth!" Chuck caught her by the shoulders. His hazel eyes sparkled with excitement. "Was the stick up and down or tipped sideways or what?"

Libby frowned, then shook her head. "I don't know. I broke it out of the ground. I don't know how it was." She felt like crying at the disappointment on Chuck's face.

114

He stood under the tree where she'd found the ring and looked slowly around him. "Look!" His voice was low and intense. "Look right over there, Elizabeth."

She frowned and looked but couldn't see what he wanted her to see. "What, Dad? What is it?"

"A ring around a stick. How about a ring around a tree? See that tree with a ring around it? Let's look around that tree."

Libby had to run to keep up with Chuck's long strides. She licked her dry lips and clasped her hands together as he looked carefully under and in the tree.

"I found something." Chuck lifted a packet down from a crotch in the tree just above the ring. "I certainly found something!"

"Open it! Oh, Dad! Open it!" Libby wanted to grab the packet out of Chuck's hands and open it.

Finally Chuck pulled the plastic cover off the packet and pulled out something. It was pictures and negatives. Chuck shook his head. "I'm glad to find these, but I was hoping for something of Brian's."

"Me too." Libby stood close to Chuck as he looked through the pictures of Pete and Lorraine. None of them showed Gary. He would be glad of that.

"Call in the gang and tell them we found what we were looking for," said Chuck tiredly. "It would have been great to find these as well as whatever Brian was trying to tell us."

115

Libby cupped her hands around her mouth and shouted for everyone to come back to the wagon. She knew they were as hot and tired as she was.

"I'll call the police and give them these just as soon as we get home." Chuck tucked the packet into his hip pocket where just the top of the packet showed. "I'll be glad to get rid of these. I would not like Pete to find these on me."

Libby shivered. She wouldn't either! She would be glad when he was arrested and put in jail.

"Did you find anything?" asked Brenda loudly. "We didn't have fun looking around. It was just a waste of time, wasn't it?"

Susan smiled and shrugged. "You all helped a lot. Ben, let's get home fast. We have a treat waiting for everyone."

Libby noticed that Chuck sat with his back against the side of the wagon. She knew he did not want anyone to notice the packet of pictures. He tried to be his usual happy self, but Libby could tell he was tense.

Just as they reached the farmyard Libby told them all how glad she was for their help and that if they'd walk to the picnic table they could have cake, ice cream, and punch.

"But the cake doesn't have candles on it," she said, laughing. "This is a 'thank you for helping' cake."

While Chuck and Ben unhitched Jack and

Dan, Libby helped Vera, Lisa, and Susan serve the food.

As the boys and girls ate, Libby saw Chuck slip in through the back door. She knew he was calling the police about the pictures. He would hide them in the house until the police came. Gary would be glad the pictures were found so Pete and Lorraine could be arrested. Maybe then he'd feel safe.

Chuck sipped his iced punch and watched the driveway for the police. Libby could see he was getting more and more impatient. Didn't the police think the pictures were very important?

Finally all the boys and girls left and Libby and Susan cleaned up the picnic table. Maybe the police would come tomorrow. Would they be this slow to arrest Pete and Lorraine?

Libby walked inside with Lisa to change Amy's diaper.

"I want to go home today, Elizabeth. I want to be home in case Brian tries to call me." Lisa pushed her blonde hair away from her tired face. She lifted her chin. "I'll take my chances with Mrs. Blevins."

"She had better not take Amy! You are a good mother."

Lisa smiled as she changed Amy. "And Brian is a good father if he would ever get home."

Chuck sat at the kitchen table as Lisa and Libby walked in to get Amy's bottle from the refrigerator. The pictures were in his hands and the plastic packet lay on the table.

Lisa stopped abruptly and stared at the packet. "Where did you get Brian's packet? He had some special pictures in it the last day he was home. He said they would bring us a lot of money."

Libby stared at Lisa, then at Chuck, then down at the packet. The pictures belonged to Brian Parr! Brian had been the man Pete Rousch was after! Libby's legs felt weak and she had to hang onto the back of a chair to stand up.

"Are you sure this is Brian's?" asked Chuck in a strange voice.

"I'm sure!" Lisa picked up the packet. "I'm positive!"

Libby slowly shook her head. How could they tell Lisa about the pictures? Brian had run from Pete Rousch. Brian had run from home. Would he run forever?

Fourteen
Brian Parr

Lisa sat on the couch next to Vera. Libby sat at Chuck's feet across from the couch. Libby could see the tears slipping down Lisa's face. She could not believe what Chuck had told her. She could not, but she was forced to. Brian had planned to blackmail Pete Rousch.

Just a few minutes ago the police had driven in to pick up the pictures. Chuck had not told them about Brian Parr.

Tears pricked Libby's eyes as she watched Lisa. Poor Lisa! What would she do now?

"Don't you understand, Vera," said Lisa, gripping Vera's hand tightly. "I must go home. Brian needs me now more than ever! What if he calls and I'm not there? I want to tell him that everything is all right." Lisa looked imploringly at Chuck. "Can't you see what must have happened? Brian couldn't go through with his plans. He knew he was wrong. Maybe he was afraid to come home. Or maybe . . . maybe he's not able to come home!" She closed her eyes and her hand fluttered at her mouth. "I will not think that he is dead or hurt!" She opened her eyes and looked directly at Chuck. "It's only seven-thirty. Please, please, will you help me move back home? I feel I must go home tonight. Maybe Brian tried to call me while I was here."

"Now, Lisa, calm down," said Vera firmly. "We'll help you move back home. But please wait until morning."

"No!" Lisa looked flushed. "I'm sorry for shouting. I must go home *now.*"

Chuck stood up and Libby jumped up beside him. "We'll get the crib loaded in the pickup. Get Amy ready."

Lisa caught his hand and squeezed it. "Thank you. Thank you!" She hugged Vera. "And thank you for helping me. I will never forget my stay here these few days. I think you helped me grow up enough to convince Mrs. Blevins that I am a fit mother."

"I'm glad I could help." Vera smiled. "I'll help you any way that I can. I love you, Lisa. You are important to me."

Lisa smiled, then hugged Vera tightly.

Libby hurried after Chuck. If she stayed with Lisa and Vera another minute she would break down and cry. And she did not want to do that!

Several minutes later Chuck, Lisa, Amy, and Libby stopped at Lisa's door. Libby had not had to talk much to convince Chuck to let her ride along. He was glad she wanted to go with him.

Carefully Chuck and Libby lifted the crib out of the back of the truck and started for the house.

Lisa stood at the door, her key in her hand, a frown on her face. Amy rested on Lisa's hip, talking and laughing. Did Amy already know this was her home? Weren't babies too little to know the difference?

"What's wrong, Lisa?" asked Chuck.

"Someone is inside the house," she whispered hoarsely, her blue eyes wide.

Libby gripped her end of the baby crib until her knuckles hurt. Maybe Pete Rousch had learned where Brian lived and come for him. Was Pete waiting inside ready to jump them? Libby trembled and almost dropped the crib.

Chuck motioned for Libby to rest the crib alongside the house. "I'll go in."

"Be careful," whispered Lisa, her face very pale.

Libby chewed the bottom of her lip. She wanted to go in with Chuck to protect him. But what could she do? And maybe he didn't need protection. Maybe mean Mrs. Blevins had found a way into the house. She might be inside looking through all the cupboards and drawers.

Chuck walked slowly into the house, leaving the door wide. "We know you're in here," he said firmly. "Come out right now."

Lisa stood at the door, trembling with fear. Suddenly her face brightened. Libby looked past her into the room. Brian Parr stood in the middle of the tiny living room. He looked as if he'd just showered and shaved. His brown eyes glowed as he saw Lisa.

"I have been trying to reach you," he said. "Oh, Lisa! I am so glad to be home!"

She ran into his arms and he hugged and kissed her, then baby Amy. Finally Lisa pulled free.

"I know about the pictures, Brian. I know about the blackmail. I would like to hear an explanation."

Brian looked quickly at Chuck and Libby. "Not now."

"We know about it, too, Brian," said Chuck. "We would like to hear your side of the story, but first help me bring in the baby crib, would you?"

Lisa couldn't take her eyes off Brian as he helped carry in the crib and set it up in Amy's tiny room.

"He's home, Elizabeth," whispered Lisa in awe. "We asked the Lord to send him home, and he answered!"

Libby smiled. Once again God had answered. How wonderful to know God loved Lisa and Brian and baby Amy! "I'm glad he's home, Lisa. I know he will have a good explanation for you."

Lisa nodded. "All that matters right now is that he's home."

Brian walked into the living room with Chuck close behind him. Brian caught Lisa's hand and pulled her down beside him on the couch, her hand tightly in his. Libby sat on the floor beside Chuck's legs.

"First, I'll tell you what we know," said Chuck. "Then you fill in the missing pieces."

Libby watched Brian and Lisa as Chuck talked. Libby could tell that Brian loved Lisa very much and that he was glad to be home. Brian was not like Libby's real dad. He had not walked out and stayed out forever. What would her life be like today if Dad had not walked out on them? She would never, never leave a husband and a baby! She would love her baby if she ever had one. She would take care of him always.

"It's your turn, Brian," said Chuck as he leaned back in his chair.

Libby watched Brian's face flush a dull red. He was ashamed of what he'd done.

"I had been sent on an assignment by the newspaper to take pictures of that warehouse because of the problems it was causing." Brian absently rubbed the back of Lisa's hand. "I was late getting there but my camera would take pictures at night so I didn't worry. At first I didn't see the man and woman there, then when I did, I decided to take pictures of them so I could have proof for the police of what they'd done." Brian took a deep breath. "I got to thinking later about what a good chance it would be to make extra money fast. And we needed it."

"Not that bad, Brian," said Lisa softly.

"I know, honey. But I wasn't thinking right. I followed them home and learned their names and address. I intended to meet them on that back road. I walked over there so I could stay out of sight until they got there. Then when I saw the man get out of the car, I panicked. I realized how wrong I'd been to think of such a terrible plan. I ran. I ran into the trees and that man was right behind me." Brian pushed his dark hair back. His brown eyes looked haunted and tired. "Suddenly I knew he was going to catch me. I could not let him get the pictures. And I could not let him learn my identity."

Brian kissed Lisa on the tip of her nose and Libby almost cried. "I knew if they found out who I was, it would cause trouble for you and Amy. I couldn't have that. I dropped my wallet in a thornbush and then hid the pictures up in a tree. I almost forgot about my class ring. I pulled it off and started to drop it, then stopped. I couldn't stand to lose it. I found a stick and slipped it on that." Brian grinned. "I left it as a clue, too. I'm glad you figured it out, Chuck."

Chuck nodded. "I'm glad Pete Rousch didn't find it and figure it out."

Libby's heart thudded hard. She could not stand to think about that.

"I knew someday you'd find the ring and give it to Lisa." Brian looked down. "I was not going to come back. But I could not stay away. I had to come home. I tried for two days to call you, honey. I got frantic when you didn't answer the

124

phone. I was afraid that Pete Rousch had found my ring and wallet and killed you and Amy.

"Today when I came past the Johnson house I saw you in their yard. I wanted to drive right in and get you but I couldn't. I . . . I was going to come home, pack some clothes, and leave again."

"No, Brian!"

"But I couldn't. I saw our things and Amy's little clothes and toys and I had to stay."

"Oh, I'm glad!"

Chuck smiled. "I think we'll need to have some long talks, Brian. But tonight you need to be alone with your family. I'm glad you were man enough to come home. Just remember that God is with you always. He is your strength."

Brian nodded. "I know. That's one of the reasons I came home when I did. I felt the Lord telling me that my place was here with Lisa and Amy. I told him I would go back if he would give me the courage. He did. And I'm here!"

"Thank the Lord!" said Lisa, leaning her head against Brian's shoulder. "And this is where we're both staying!"

"But not us," said Chuck, grinning. He stood up and held his hand out to Libby. "It's time for us to go home, Elizabeth."

Libby jumped to her feet and slipped her hand in Chuck's. "Good night, Brian and Lisa. I'm glad you're both happy."

"Me too," said Lisa. "Thanks again, Elizabeth, for all your help."

"You're welcome, Lisa." Libby smiled up at Chuck. "It's time to go home, Dad. Tomorrow Susan and I have another birthday party, a birthday party without any strange happenings."

"You hope," said Chuck with a wide grin.

"I *know*," said Libby. It felt wonderful to have Chuck tease her. She squeezed his hand. "We have the rest of the summer to have perfect birthday parties."